D1409594

NEW DIRECTIONS 44

In memoriam
EUGENIO MONTALE
1896–1981

XENIA

Nobody could write about you
the way you wrote about Mosca,
after she died.
There couldn't be another *Xenia*.
You yourself couldn't do it, were you
to write your own obituary
while still alive.

—G. Singh

ND

New Directions in Prose and Poetry 44

Edited by J. Laughlin

with Peter Glassgold and Frederick R. Martin

A New Directions Book

Library of Congress Catalog Card Number: ~~37-1751~~ 00-9047

ACKNOWLEDGMENTS
Grateful acknowledgment is made to the editors and publishers of books and magazines in which some of the material in this volume first appeared: for John Allman, *Friends of George Sand Newsletter;* for Allen Grossman, *Canto* and *Salmagundi* (Copyright © 1981 by Allen Grossman); for James Purdy, *The Niagara Magazine* (Copyright © 1980 by The Niagara Magazine).

Kerry Shawn Keys' translation of "A Knife All Blade" by João Cabral de Melo Neto was originally published in a limited edition by Pine Press, Camp Hill, Pennsylvania (Copyright © 1980 by Kerry Shawn Keys).

"My Mother Walked Out" by Michael Hannon first appeared as separate chapbooks published in limited editions by Rainbow Resin Press, Grover City, California (Copyright © 1977 by Rainbow Resin Press) and Turkey Press, Isla Vista, California (Copyright © 1978 by Michael Hannon).

Sections V and XXXVII of H. D.'s "Vale Ave" originally appeared in *Poetry* (Copyright © 1957 by the Estate of Hilda Doolittle). Section XVIII was first published in *The Atlantic* (Copyright © 1958 by the Estate of Hilda Doolittle).

Excerpts from Edmond Jabès' *Yaël* (© Éditions Gallimard 1967), in translations by Rosmarie Waldrop, appear by permission of the publisher, Éditions Gallimard, Paris.

Manufactured in the United States of America
First published clothbound (ISBN: 0-8112-0838-9) and as New Directions Paperback 537 (ISBN: 0-8112-0839-7) in 1982
Published simultaneously in Canada by George J. McLeod, Ltd., Toronto

New Directions Books are published for James Laughlin
by New Directions Publishing Corporation,
80 Eighth Avenue, New York 10011

CONTENTS

GEORGE SAND AT PALAISEAU (1865)

JOHN ALLMAN

August

For the moment, no bad odor. Limbs bend. Eyes stare
toward the memory of the hand
closing them. She washes him quickly, changes
his nightgown; plants flowers between the rim of his body
and August air,
faithful Alexandre.
He'd said nothing when she ran off with Marchal.
How he whimpered in the cold bath, telling her
to continue Fuster's
treatment, saddened
by the burden he was for Madame. Fifteen years,
still he would not use *tu*. Did she ever love a man
not frail? His hand,
thin as light, lifting
a gesture to the window, sliding beyond her grasp.
Wheat fields, bloodied by sun, streaming toward Paris.

What will she write without him? Advice to new friends?
Flaubert would redo the scene,
rearrange the pillows, have a cart rumble
into a rut, put the window on the west wall,
lamplight falling obliquely
on a youthful face.

She listens to birds. The cook's clatter. Downstairs,
last week, his sister held her ears, while he inhaled
the *gaz*. She remembers
Valdemosa; Chopin's pallid
hand fading into Études, while she wrote furiously,
her study a fumoir; workmen shaking their heads
after hauling the piano
up the mountain;
the smell of fish, olive oil, garlic oozing
like salt from the walls, from a thrashing sea.

She's finished the novel, *Le Bonheur*, left intact
the bits of dialogue Alexandre
contrived. *Their* novel, to give him something
of life, in making art. She reads her diary entry:
"The will to heal
is all." Was he the oaf
her son, Maurice, called him? He seems perfectly
quiet. He'd won some of the arguments, rewritten
some of the parts
for the puppet shows
at Nohant. And she sewed clothes, the tiny
trousers, while friends argued across the room
with the dancing
marionettes. A son's jealousy
swells like the Indre, swirls a muddy water
about her thighs. Lovers are swept away like debris.

Men say she talks like a man, the odor of cigars
in her hair,
clinging to her dress, the stink of equality.
What a husband forgets, a son picks up as his own:
Maurice, imminent
landlord of Nohant, seigneur
of orchards, pavilion and woods, telling her she's
too old. For two nights, she sits near the body,
mourning little Nini
and Cocoton, the grandchildren
also gone. The cupboard of her hearing about to close,

how long will she write of love? Visitors arrive, but
            not upstairs: his sister weeping,
            fearing the dead face. The church will not
bless his ground. She must carry him into plain earth.
"Do not worry. I shall not be ill. I refuse to be ill."

November

In the morning, autumn glistens. Alexandre's presence,
            as in life, recedes, allowing her
to be herself. It was good to be in Paris, the Odéon,
Théâtre-Français, where the voice carries out of Nature
            the passion life cannot
            afford. Perhaps, she'll write
Marchal; tell how blood rises, old women clutch
their shawls, remembering the long hands of Liszt.
            Her mood is for children's
            tales. At night, crisp
emanations of the stars. Recently, at dawn, mist
rolling through trees, fluency returned: ten pages,
            and birds
            flapping into the wet air.
She emerges from the cloud of cigarette smoke, someone's
Muse, but does not find him etching, dark eyes dilating.

Marchal, fat darling, this morning in Paris, an early
            breakfast, someone else
in your arms, what do you remember of art?
It's a new age, seeking hardness; Flaubert's music
            of objects.
            Poor Marie, beloved Dorval,
that full voice breaking over an audience of stones.
"Dear Gustave, what are you doing?—grinding away,
            I fancy, you, in solitude too . . .
            mother probably in Rouen. Do you
sometimes spare a thought for 'the old troubadour
of the ale-house clock, who sings, and will always sing
            of perfect love'?"
            The wind creaks toward winter,

sweeping voices aloft, an opera of the damned. Who will
write of her? The peasants of La Châtre? A drunken mayor?

No one believes in her minor aches—as if she owned
        more than her reputation,
with Solange, her daughter, the slut of Europe!
The lead weight of the Second Empire still keeps wives
        in place. Let the lovers
        enter their fiacres,
drive south away from husbands who tattle in books
about nothing. In old age, a new magnetism: the moon
        drawing up the vapors
        of a ragged field,
pulling at her blood, tugging the half-surfaced soul
that keeps going under. In abstinence, a red death.
        Marchal, huge springtime,
        we grow plump, and France
lacks exaltation. How many dinners purchase a hug?
I'm an infant, without sex or energy, blinking at the dark.

She pulls at her hair, remembering how she'd cut it off
        and sent it in a box
to Musset, a final blow. Poor Alfred, on the crossing
to Genoa, groaning in his cabin, sick as a girl.
        She wrote for hours,
        stood on deck, took sea-spray
full in the eyes. How would Delacroix paint her now?
All lines, without color, changing his art
        because she did not
        remain young?
She can still look to heaven, hands clasped, face
pale in its own light. She can still hear Balzac
        huffing up the stairs,
        hugging loaves of bread
for Jules and the runaway Aurore. She hears mice. A faint
scratching at her heart. Things from God that must return.

A WINTER DEATH

MICHAEL McGUIRE

A friend of a former client met at a cocktail party had invited the lawyer up here. And, for some reason, perhaps because he was a little at a loss after winding up his practice, on the spur of the moment (unusual for him) he had accepted and decided to come up for the weekend. The client's friend was an artist, and above the fine hardwood floors of his house, his original works covered the walls. Also present were a friend of the artist, who was a potter, and the potter's wife and the artist's wife. The still young wives had known each other before (in fact, this was the reason for the continued association of the couples); oddly enough, they had once danced together in scanty, sequined outfits, with feathers covering their breasts and pink hearts, like valentines, concealing their vaginas; they had been oggled together by drunken businessmen, and together they had mugged and aped the corny sight gags that insured their return engagements. These facts had been revealed to the lawyer, and not *sotto voce,* by the potter's wife.

Now the two women sat quietly talking in the artist's winter vacation home. Beyond the double plate-glass windows snow fell silently. The artist's wife's young daughter practiced her *grands battements* at the *barre* in tiny black tights. Her small swinging foot scuffed the floor regularly, like a pendulum that would not be still. Occasionally she looked at herself, almost blankly, in the floor-length mirror. And, from time to time, her mother looked at her.

It was a late Sunday morning. The three men sat in soft, widely separated chairs by the empty fireplace. Though the central heat was on, the huge stones of the fireplace looked cold and the smell of last night's blaze was still strong in the air. The floor around them was littered with discarded magazines and toys, and the inner surface of the immense windows was gray wtih cigarette smoke. Later in the day, after a walk together upon the cold, inhospitable beach—which always seemed at this time of year, the artist said, to want to be alone—they would go their separate ways. From his seat the lawyer could see the artist's picture of his wife: small and dark, hanging unevenly between the kitchen and the hall, not much more than a scribble in never-finished charcoal, as if the artist had tried, tried hard to complete it, but had somehow not been able to. Yet it was her.

"Look at these hands," said the artist, spreading his large-knuckled, almost oversize hands for all to see. "Meant for working the land, you think? Perhaps there really is peasant blood back there, but sculpture was my love. My love," he repeated. "Yet somehow, after I began to teach, there was never time. And that was twenty years ago. Even if I were . . . to go back . . . I wonder if I could lift the hammer or even hold the chisel now." He paused and looked around him. "Now I look at my land, I watch my children grow; we cut our Christmas tree together . . ."

The potter and the lawyer looked at the tree: huge for its purpose, now more or less denuded, dried out and shedding profusely, it lay on its side by the door ready to be dragged outside again and burnt in the spring.

"You sure you found that tree on your land?" inquired the potter shrewdly. "I noticed a nasty looking stump on the walk over here—well within my acres."

"I'll show you the spot," laughed the artist. "It was a hell of a trek dragging that tree, even with all of us pulling."

As they bantered the lawyer's mind wandered to the night before when, content just to be there in a new environment, at a little distance, listening to the voices, he had sat close to the roaring fire, his drink cradled in his hand, and separating herself from the smoke and the murmer, the artist's wife had seemed to materialize close at hand and sat down next to him. He acknowledged her presence, and then his eyes returned to the fire. They sat some time without speaking. Now and then her youngest daughter would sidle up to have her mouth wiped or to raise her shirt and display her tiny, swelling belly as if she, in her turn, were already heavy with another, smaller version of herself. And in the moments of relative solitude, the artist's wife had seemed to be talking to him alone, and he (an older man?) had been content to listen.

"I took a year off once," she said, "from everything. It wasn't that long ago. I lived in a hole in dirty, gray New York. I never made a meal. I'd eat standing up, the bag from the grocery store on the counter right beside me. But I was alone!" she said, leaning closer, her voice thick with relief. "Do you know what that is: not even a dog or a sleeping child; no door opening, no sound of feet coming toward you, no . . . breathing? I hesitate to call myself anything," she added quietly, looking more into the fire than at him, "but I do paint. And that was the year of the seven-foot canvases." She had paused. "Now I teach. We all teach. There is a very businesslike atmosphere in the classroom. I teach the technology of it. The word 'art' never crosses my lips. I have tenure," she had said, looking more than ever like her portrait.

Now the men's conversation was over. Now it was time to drive down for a final walk along the beach. And the artist and his wife, and the potter and his wife, and the lawyer walked along the beach. This time it was colder than the woods, the north wind blowing down the east-facing, deserted stretch of sand, and the sun was already out of sight behind the trees to the southwest. But, though the landward view was dark, cold-looking, the sea was bright and alive and indifferent to the discomfort of the walkers, and its light graceful motion actively reflected the fast-fading, deep, cerulean blue above it.

As they walked northward into the wind along the great flat expanse, tears were forced to their eyes, and at times they seemed to be blown apart, leaving each alone for a while with his own body and the cold, and then to come together again. A gull cried overhead. In the distance an old reddish coaster or fishing boat seemed to be moving aimlessly up and down, making little, if any, progress on a sea of azure brightness. More or less pointed toward the land, it never reached it while they were there, and moving at different speeds themselves, they were soon well-separated specks on the already colorless extent of sand.

The artist and the lawyer, struggling far in front of the others, and neither ready to admit that his heart was hammering, his breath short, and his face and hands nearly frozen, at length came to a stop together and turned downwind to relieve themselves. Even that operation was difficult with numb fingers, but a chill went out of the shoulder blades with the released pressure, and a reassuring steam was briefly visible.

"Tell me," asked the artist manfully, "what do you see when you look out across this land?"

The lawyer raised his eyes and saw several moving forms, central among them the artist's wife, the configuration that had got her her first job noticeable even at this distance, her lovely girl children moving away from her and back to her as if they were on rubber bands.

"When I first stood here," continued the artist, "when I first saw the winter clouds reflected on the flat wet sand, I knew I had never seen anything like it, that I never would again. But there is no adequate response. When I stand here again after I've been away, I can't believe it was ever like this or, at least, that I had ever seen it. This must be some land I'm not supposed to enter."

Suddenly the wind dropped and the sound of voices carried to them across the sand. And for a moment the lawyer thought he heard the artist's wife laughing. He had not heard her laugh before, and his eyes opened a little wider at the sound. It may have been a bird flying somewhere out of sight, but at that distance, before the wind returned, he was just able to convince himself that he had truly heard her laughter, and even seen her laughing face.

Now, in silent agreement, the two men began to let the wind push them down the beach toward the scattered figures, the car, the women and children growing in the distance. "I know," the artist was saying: "You're tired of the smoke in your lungs, or the sound of feet and the mumble of massed voices. Well, you're perfectly welcome to stay, I mean in this part of the country, if you can find a place. See what you think of it after we've flocked back to our institutions, and you're left alone with the people who sell the groceries and pump the gas and fill the holes in the roads and put the telephone lines back up after a storm. See what you think."

In time the lawyer, perhaps for the second time in his life following an impulse, did learn what it was like to be alone there. The holi-

and even a book of poems, a young man's poems, the occasional line of which he would ponder at length in his head. And before he turned the light out, it felt to him as if not just the household and the port but the entire world was sleeping peacefully. In the darkness the cold seemed to tighten its grip on the house, forcing all sorts of unidentifiable sounds from the old structure, but beneath the heaped covers he was safe as a child. And in the morning he sometimes managed a walk to the point of land before breakfast, sometimes in time to see the sun rising out of the sea.

Weeks passed. Of the few people around, none seemed interested in him, and he, on his part, did not venture to speak with anyone. What a change it was from the social contacts and obligations he had known. And yet, strangely enough perhaps, he experienced no restlessness or even loneliness. A necessary time of silence he began to consider it and thought of the earth resting underneath the snow. Yet March came with its winds and changeable weather, and still he had no urge to go. At times he puzzled over this fact; he knew he did not have centuries ahead of him like the fallow land.

And he began to wonder why, really, he had come, and why he stayed on. Without many articles of faith, it had always seemed to him, in retrospect, that everything had had to happen just as it did. Now something in him had changed. He was aware of that. But why, and for what? At times he would think of working, of keeping up his contacts and holding onto his clients after all. Then he would sit down at the tiny, almost child-size desk in his room, arrange the blank paper neatly before him, and hold a full pen over it. But he could not even bring himself to cross off the old address of his printed letterhead and write in his new, temporary one.

Then he would close all in his desk drawer and walk, and as he walked, always trying to extend his range by ever so little, it might occur to him to take up some cause before it was too late, to devote his energies. But just the thought of returning to the airless courtroom would leave him with a faint nausea. And occasionally, walking on the long, deserted beach where he and the artist had first left their footprints, he would become aware of how keenly he looked into the clear distance through the cold, salt air, as if he were on the lookout for a beached whale or the rockets from a dramatically wrecked ship. But there was only the recurring, variable weather and now familiar pattern of nights and days.

And, as the cold seemed gradually to release its grip, he found he could walk further and further each day until he was covering ten miles. What would his fellow New Yorkers say to that? And instead of hard gray pavement, he had the changing earth to walk upon; and instead of weak, unwilling legs, tired in a block, his legs swung out easily from his hips mile after mile: he found he had increased his stride and found a rhythm in walking which he fell into as soon as he left the house and started down the beach. Days passed, and the miles he had never covered before fell one by one behind him.

One day, on which the sun seemed to be seriously beginning to reassert itself, he followed the winding road out to the artist's house, perhaps simply because it was a destination, a goal. After a few miles further than he was used to, and at least one wrong turn, he came to a stop before it on healthily tired legs. The house confronted him, shuttered and deserted looking, its weathered wood almost the color of the cold muddy forest floor. There had been a steady rise in the land from the sea to the house, and he stood a moment, realizing how much further he really had come than he was used to. A dark cloud slid across the sun and, at the same time, a chill wind rustled through the trees which still held a few of last year's darkened, brittle leaves. He shivered involuntarily, and an unfastened shutter on the "old-fashioned" side of the house banged desolately.

Walking up to the house to fix it, he thought he could smell the damp ashes of an extinguished fire, and at the uncovered window he took the liberty of cupping his hands against the glass and looking in. His heart nearly stopped: only inches from his own an expressionless face seemed to be looking right through him. He started back, half aware of a look of shock and horror on his own face, and only as a reflection of sky and branches returned to the glass did he recognize, almost as an afterthought, the artist's wife. Partially recovering himself, yet still somehow apprehensive, he knocked, almost absurdly he felt, on the door, knowing there could be no answer. And, after a moment, he tried it, and finding it open, stepped in and shut the door behind him.

With only the occasional half-light from the single, unfastened shutter, it was necessary to stand a moment before proceeding. There was an airless, soundless quality to the semidarkness, and the penetrating cold was that of a deserted house. His footsteps sounded almost too slow, too casual as he advanced into the main room: the sound of a returning criminal, he thought for no reason, of a criminal returning to the scene of a crime which he had no reason to fear would ever be discovered and for which no alibi would ever be necessary. There was no telling how long the fire had been out; there was no wood; the artist's wife sat in a straight-backed chair before the empty fireplace. She had wrapped a blanket around herself; there was an empty cigarette pack and a glassful of ashes on the floor beside her.

The shutter banged open, and he noticed the rest of the furniture lined against the walls and covered with sheets. Somehow unwilling to approach the artist's wife directly, he walked around in front of her. Moving through the still air of the house, it seemed colder than outside. Her body hidden beneath the blanket, she seemed without form or shape. She did not look at him when he stood in front of her, and it occurred to him that, if she were to look up suddenly, his hair might stand on end.

"I didn't think there was anyone here," he said.

The shutter almost closed, then didn't and again banged open against the wall.

Without looking at him she exhaled briefly, as though she had thought of laughing at something to herself, but her laugh had gotten no further than that.

"Maybe there isn't," she said suddenly and without looking at him, the words seeming hardly to leave her lips.

All at once, and for no reason, he was angry.

"You're a young woman," he said abruptly.

She looked at him then, almost as if she were showing him that there was nothing at all in her eyes.

"What are you doing to yourself?" he said, too loudly. "What's happened?"

His words echoed meaninglessly. For a moment she seemed to see him, then he felt the vision of himself fading from her eyes. He waited, looking at her, imagining events a lawyer might be equipped to deal with. A minute passed, and then another. He had the feeling she would not object no matter how long he stood there looking at her. Her motionless face was, at that moment, a perfect picture of herself, the kind you come to a stop before and don't leave without looking back at several times. He felt himself hesitating between alternatives, but when he did walk away from her she did not turn her head. And outside, looking at the road, it occurred to him just to forget he had found anyone here and to go back the way he had come. Instead he found the ax and split some logs and came back and started a fire in the big fireplace. She had not changed her position when he returned. She neither moved nor watched him as he built the fire.

He learned quickly enough that there was no power in the house and no way of cooking except in the fireplace, where he managed to hang a kettle, peasant fashion, on a chain over the open flames. The fire was beginning to give some heat, and she seemed, in a somewhat puzzled way, to be looking at it. While the water was heating he went back outside and repaired the shutter. The wind had continued to blow, and one cloud had followed another across the low gray sky. It seemed to him, looking up, that the day had disappeared somewhere, morning proceeding directly into night. He fastened several other shutters open and returned to the somewhat lightened house just as the big kettle was beginning to steam and spit. Lifting it off the chain with a rag, he carried it to the kitchen where he located the tea and the pot. He discovered a tin of milk and an old box of sugar cubes in a cabinet and added enough of each to a cup to give her some strength. When he returned, he found her holding out her hands to the fire.

"Here." He handed her the tea.

She stared at it a moment, then slowly took it. He went back to the kitchen and poured himself a cup, then carried the kettle back in and set it near the fire, where it would stay warm. Not bothering to take the sheet off one of the large chairs, he shoved it nearer the fire and, making no attempt to move her, sat in it himself. After a moment he looked at her. She held the full cup with both hands wrapped around it, her elbows and knees close together as she hunched toward the flames. It seemed a long time before she tasted it again, this time looking down at it. She said something, but it was spoken too softly for him to hear what it was, and he didn't want to ask her to repeat it.

The rectangles of the windows began to darken. Now and then a fitful cold wind made a circle of the house, as if trying to find a way in. No one drove up the road or down it, for the season was neither one thing nor the other and the houses were without function and empty. He must have drowsed off briefly, not knowing how tired he really was. When he opened his eyes the fire had gone down and she was on her knees in front of it, carefully and silently rebuilding it. Aware of an unaccustomed lassitude in his body, he made no move to help her and simply watched. When the fire was blazing again, she went back to her chair.

Again they sat without speaking. With her hands lightly clasped in her lap, she seemed to be almost philosophically observing each flare-up and collapse in the structure of burning wood. Later, as the walls darkened and the wind again circled the house, flinging itself now at the door, now at the windows, it was his turn to rebuild and rekindle. Then he too returned to his chair. A lifetime might have passed since he started out from his room by the sea. But no one would miss him or come looking for him, any more than anyone from the city had. And what did it matter? Silence moved through his body like the warmth from the fire. Everything that had ever happened to him had happened so long ago it was difficult to remember a single incident, a single face. It seemed that he might have been married to this woman since she had come of age, might have known her a thousand times, and with the strong, never fully given love in him have kept this night forever at bay.

He woke to find the windows on one side of the house already light, the sky beyond them silvery gray. He looked at his watch without moving. Dawn. He did not remember falling asleep, but the sleep before dawn was always best, magical and full of dreams, as if already touched by the sun, still just out of sight and moving toward him. His face against the back of the chair, he found himself already missing the new routine of his nights and days, his attic room, and the still sleeping port. Perhaps now it was time to head quietly back down to the sea: once round the port, to the point of land—then into breakfast. His hand moving down his side in preparation for rising encountered something unfamiliar, held it, and lifted it. He looked down. He saw in one glance that the blanket was on him and that her chair was empty.

He stood up slowly, feeling the stiffness in his legs, and folded the still warm blanket. It seemed so much a part of her that he was just tempted to sniff it primitively, but he set the folded blanket on the chair. The fire had only recently gone out, and the room was still warm. Not finding the artist's wife in the kitchen and expecting her to appear eventually from the bathroom, he stepped outside himself only to be surprised by the unseasonable return of winter: hard, driven flakes rushed past the house. Already several inches of snow on the ground were staring back at a low, dark sky. After standing a moment behind a tree, he went back inside. He stood by the fireplace for several minutes, as though waiting at the spot where he had last seen her was sure to bring her out. There was not the faintest sound within the house, and the wind seemed to be whirling almost victoriously around it.

It took him only a second to step into the tiny hallway and observe the empty bathroom and two small, empty bedrooms, their flat, striped mattresses uncovered from Christmas to summer. He stepped once more into the kitchen, walking more quickly now, his body seeming to know by itself that it could move as it pleased, and his boots sounded loudly in the empty house. There was no one in the kitchen, of course, only a washed glass upside down drying on the sink.

Closing his coat carefully about him and pulling his hat down over his ears, he went outside again. This time he felt the door lock behind him when he closed it, and standing there on the snow-covered step, this time looking for signs or evidence, he at once saw what he had not noticed before: her small, light footprints leading to the road. Apparently she had gone soon after it had begun to snow: there were only the slightest indentations in the smooth, white surface, as if only her spirit had walked there. He followed the footprints out to the road. A highway department or telephone company truck, or both, had passed. On the road there was no way of knowing which way she had gone—up: toward where the road ended in the hills after the last empty house; or down: to cars, stores, the bus station.

He stood there, perhaps hoping to see her small figure on the road getting larger, and he remembered the scene on the beach: her girl children moving away from her and back, her laugh he thought he had heard. He stood there, the flakes rushing down the road past him, until one arm and one leg were nearly white and his feet were as void of feeling as the roots of trees beneath the frozen earth. The trucks did not pass or return. Perhaps she had ridden off in one. The air grew white around him, the snow falling thicker and faster, blowing almost horizontally past him, one side of his face already having little more feeling than his feet. He pictured the artist's wife in an overheated bus headed south. At times he could almost see her face in the whirling snow.

Eventually he had no choice but to continue down the road himself. After a few minutes moving at his own pace, he had warmed up. He stopped to brush the snow from his arm and leg and, starting again, the wind at his back and the way tending downhill, he was even enjoying the unseasonable storm driving past him. His last taste of winter, he told himself, as if the purpose of the weather was to fix its impressions upon him, and he found himself thinking of the artist's wife in New York. He imagined her blown around some windy corner at him: she is moving rapidly, brightly, a large canvas under her arm. She sees him. There is the moment of recognition, her lips opening . . . But no, of course; he realizes it is impossible: she doesn't know him, he doesn't know her. They pass each other without a word.

As if in a final, triumphant fling, the storm settled down in earnest around him. At a division in the road he even chose the wrong way, perhaps unconsciously attempting to keep the storm at his back. This road narrowed and dropped away suddenly and, becoming aware of the unfamiliarity of his surroundings, he stopped and was about to fight his way back up to the right turning, when something to the side caught his eye.

She was sitting very still in a sheltered spot, her back against one of the few large trees. It was the brightness of her coat that he had noticed, even though it was partly concealed by snow. He practically had to wade over to her through the fallen branches. Again she was facing somewhat away from him. Standing at her side, he touched her shoulder. He removed his gloves and placed the backs of his fingers gently against her cheek. He took her face in both hands. Then, slipping them behind her neck, underneath her soft hair, he put his own face against hers, moving it lightly over her eyes, her mouth, speaking her name just loudly enough for her to hear. But her head did not move, her eyes did not open. Putting his arms around her he tried to lift her, but the stiffness in her body resisted him.

He stood looking at her. She looked just like a child sitting in the snow. And he . . . ? He was an older man. Around them, between them, the gray flakes fell.

VALE AVE

H. D.

To: Amico.
Küsnacht, Spring 1957

This sequence introduces Adam's first wife, Lilith. Is she the Serpent who tests the *androgynat primordial?* Serpent (*saraph*), it is said, has the same root derivation as Seraph, so Lilith may be Serpent or Seraph, as Adam, whom we invoke as Lucifer, the Light-bringer, in his pre-Eve manifestation, may be Angel or Devil.

The Lucifer-Lilith, Adam-Eve formula may be applied to all men and women, though here we follow the *processus* through the characters of Elizabeth and Sir Walter, meeting and parting, *Vale Ave,* through time—specifically, late Rome, dynastic Egypt, legendary Provence, early seventeenth-century England, and contemporary London. She is the niece of the Elizabethan poet and alchemist Sir Edward Dyer. Sir Walter secretly and mysteriously becomes her lover during the last months of his life in the Tower of London. After his death, Elizabeth recalls him to her, through her uncle's Art and through the alchemy of memory. Sir Walter was himself an alchemist, as history tells us, and Elizabeth identifies herself with him, although:

> I hardly knew my Lord, true we had met
> in sudden frenzy, parted in the dark,
> and all the rest was mystery and a portent.

Mystery and a portent, yes, but at the same time, there is Resurrection and the hope of Paradise.

I

We would name you Light-bearer,
pre-Adamic, of the sacred *Luciferum*,

no Dark Majesty but Light-bringer,
an Angel as God first created you,

for it is true that I called to you,
it is true that you answered,

"it was no serpent that God cursed,
it was Adam's first wife, Lilith,

who spoke in the Tree"; was Lucifer, Adam,
was Adam, Lucifer, torn asunder,

one Adam for Eve, one for Lilith,
his first wife, a being, an entity

born of no man-rib but a Tree;
Lucifer and Lilith, to taste no bitter fruit,

nor toil nor bear children,
but to remember, only to remember . . .

II

"Cursed shall she be,
the Voice within the Tree,"
but for how long?

True, I was a long time there,
Carthage, Rome, Tyre,
while you ploughed the earth, implacable,

Hannibal, Caesar, Martel;
those chains could never hold,
the pit was never closed,

but a volcano made earth uninhabitable,
here, there; there, here;
but still enchantment rose

out of the sea, when in the centurion's tent,
or by the dunes, or in a fisher's hut,
following, inexorable destiny, we met.

III

For us, no open door
to hearth and the hearth-fire,
the moment before, the long rest after,

but immediacy, urgency—awake? asleep?—
a chasm, a cave, a monstrous fissure
in time, a breaking of law,

time-sequence, star-sequence;
the sun stands still,
the moon unveiled, revealed,

forgets to draw the tides;
the earth will shiver and break
if we hesitate—asleep? awake?

IV

Yet sometimes, I would sweep the floor,
I would put daisies in a tumbler,
I would have long dreams before, long daydreams after,

There would be no gauntleted knock on the door,
or tap-tap with a riding crop,
no galloping here and back,

but the latch would softly lift,
would softly fall,
dusk would come slowly,

and even dusk could wait
till night encompasses us;
dawn would come gracious, not too soon,

day would come late,
and the next day and the next,
while I found pansies to take the place of daisies,

and a spray of apple blossom after that,
no calendar of fevered hours,
Carthago delenda est and the Tyrian night.

V

O, we were penitent enough, God knows,
you wore the Nessus' tunic,
I, the rose with nails for petals,

underneath my robe; I pressed
the seven swords of Mary to my heart,
within the hollow of my wounded breasts;

I walked, numb with the incense,
never passed a friar or priest or brother,
but my glance fell to the pavement,

but the very stones of the cathedral floor
bore imprint of your sandals;
I must close my eyes and stare

at the rose window, but the rose betrayed,
the glow of green and azure set aflame
the row of kings and saints along the wall,

the stone-story of Creation and the Fall;
O, we were penitent enough, God knows,
but how revoke decrees made long ago?

VI

The candle swells with weight of its own fervor,
the melting wax runs down,
to fill the hollow of the candleholder,

and as it flames with headier heat and headier,
it seems to blaze with iridescent splendor
that I may never look upon,

prostrated as I am, in adoration;
the lashes of my eyes are wet,
my swollen eyelids burn;

dear Lord, how long can I endure,
my cold hands clasped, my numb knees
frozen on this chapel floor?

VII

Go now, my love, the cock has crowed again,
go now, my love, dawn touches the windowframe,
go now, my love, your face is haggard and worn,

tell to your waiting brothers, you had sworn
to do your triple penance, say, all night long,
you flayed your worn flesh, Our Lord witnesses it,

go, go my love, I join my sisters now,
trembling and weak; dear sister, one will say,
you must not try the flesh unutterably,

but if I must, I must, I'll answer her;
go now, for it is day, or soon will be,
and we will take our place within the row,

of kneeling worshipers and penitants,
and we will vow again, our ancient vow,
at matins; it is day, go, go.

VIII

Our ancient—vow within the purple tent
I lay alone; he left a goblet (spiced with—what?)
within my reach; all day the village burned;

have he and his few, strength to drive them back,
or will they throng, beasts in their wild-beast pelts,
great bearded giants with their threatening horns,

will they swoop and tear me, helpless, hapless here,
will they stare and laugh,
see what has stricken Rome,

will they leer and ask in their barbaric speech,
which is best, to take her in a cage
or burn her here; will they keep

a naked, unkempt Lilith for a show
for witches and young women with fair hair?
Will he return? I have not strength to stand.

IX

Keep Lilith in a cage, curse Lilith in a Tree?
no; no barbaric hordes nor gods can yet prevail
against the law that drags the snail across the grass,

that turns the falcon from his course,
that drives the lion until he finds
the lioness within the cave;

men gave new names to us, many names, fabulous,
but Lilith was the first that God cursed outright,
and Lucifer's became that sinister name,

while man himself rebelled and fabricated meteor and flame,
such as the thunder once alone proclaimed,
"death-dealing such as this, comes but from God";

could *aves* and could prayers control
these man-made meteors, God knows
I would be penitent enough and crawl

in sackcloth on my bleeding knees;
but those prayers are worn threadbare;
there must be others, bright with vivid fire,

revolatilizing, luminous, life-bearing
and light-bringing, to compel a Star, Lucifer,
to return and save mankind.

X

"They drive them past the riverbank," he said;
I must have slept, the air was soft and cool,
he stood in his blue tunic; had he come

some hour or some half-hour before I woke?
"does Octavius keep your armor in his tent?"
he said, "I let Octavius take my place,"

(he never left his men), "and are there others here?"
I asked; "they will come later," and he took the goblet
and turned it slowly, "then, you swallowed this?"

"perhaps, I can't remember"; "there was only
the poppy-juice, the opiate in the wine,
I left for sleep"; "and you are tired," I said;

"no, never half so glad, so wide awake," he led
me to the open space before the tent, and far I saw and far,
the peaceful contour of the winding river,

and levels where the villages had been;
it must have rained, there was no smoke,
no breath of smoldering timbers, it was clear

and stars were as snow drifting in mid-air . . .
we seemed one flambeau for the world to see,
we did not even know that we were dead.

XI

And those we left? Hermas comes first,
he made a garden on the Aventine;
my Lord, how is it, I remember this,

for suddenly (whose fault?) we find ourselves
crowded against a bulwark on a wharf,
buffeted by alien winds—take cover—

whose the shout—whose ships—whose men,
my Lord, why are we here—why do you shudder—
am I stronger then, than you

who played the god before all men?
where are we—and what threatens—
are you the enemy, are they seeking you

with lanterns on the quay
and sentries on the breakwater?
O, do not tear yourself away,

for if they take you, I am lost again;
where did we come from—how did we meet here—
where have you gone—

dear Lord, and is this all that I have left,
only this empty, old discarded cloak?
my alien garments weigh my limbs like lead,

when I would run—
Ave Maria—save us,
Christ who saves.

XII

It filtered through, though it was lies, I knew,
he had been stretched upon the rack and tried,
condemned and died;

"no, no, he was beheaded: he did not swing
at Tyburn, as they say," "but quiet, quiet, Peter,
the Lady Elizabeth may overhear";

"tell her to go—some saw her on the quay—
and go yourself, I'll stay on at the Tower,"
(I crouched upon the landing of the upper stair),

"the gates are closed or will be before day,
I have the Tower passes and the key; Agatha, go";
"they will not want us, Peter, at the Manor,

with all this talk of plague"; "but they are
Christian folk and she is kin, make ready,
she is weak, some say, with child,

although her Lord left here, a year ago—"
"hist—he returned and made a secret visit,
on the Queen's business—" "you know he died of fever,

in New Spain"; "no matter; how can I drag her away;
to her, the very paving stones are sacred
and London is a holy city to her."

XIII

I can not remember, only that my name
was Elizabeth Dyer; I can not remember my husband,
only my lover; I faintly remember old nurse Agatha

and her husband, who had been our house-servant
and now carried a halberd at the Tower;
I can not remember how we got away,

I can remember a dead child but I never saw it,
and maybe, it wasn't dead, after all,
I was too ill to remember;

Agatha was herself, a Tower, things were hidden
under flowing mantles, in those days,
and strange, alien farthingales, and Agatha put me to bed, anyway;

I was delirious and I talked (she said) of a purple tent,
and men with horns (devils, she thought, I meant)
and stars and lilies and the Aventine.

XIV

I had my mother's Missal, but the prayers
fluttered against the dark and broke and fell,
for this too, was anathema and cursed,

the good Queen had instructed all of us,
to do away with painted images,
the breviary and the Latin and the Mass;

but there were furtive, secret worshipers,
we were suspect, in that I shared the curse
that fell upon my Lord and atheists;

Hieronymos, pity us, Agnes, Lucy, help;
the very names were potent but they fluttered,
fell and broke, like aimless birds, lost

on a continent that lured them north,
that later, in the winter, would have drawn them back
to sun and sand, the Mystery and Egypt.

XV

I hardly knew my Lord, true we had met
in sudden frenzy, parted in the dark,
and all the rest was mystery and a portent;

none had stood higher in the Queen's respect,
name England and you know his name,
Agatha sheltered us, he came and went;

no shadow followed us until the last;
I drew him to me through my uncle's Art,
though I knew little of it, at his death,

he named the Seraphim, the future would encompass us,
separate yet together with their wings;
he said "Sir Edward Dyer's niece?

"You mean that Edward Dyer who was disgraced?
an alchemist who told the Queen the truth?
but where is she?" somehow he found me out;

perhaps it was not difficult, "her name, her reputation?"
"almost a nun; she lives with two old servants
near the Tower; her husband's in New Spain."

XVI

They spoke his name across the candles,
the goblets stood unmoving on the table
and the table stood and those same cups

I always loved, the fruit bowl, the decanter;
the candleflames burned straight, they never moved,
I thought an earthquake shook the house

but it was I who trembled when my uncle spoke,
(the candleflames burned straight, they never moved),
"you must have heard talk of this in the town";

my cousin answered, "let her forget the town—
they said, he bribed the gatekeepers,
and came and went out of the Tower,

but never far; they even say
he could have got away by sea,
but honored his *parole*";

(and now the wind was beating in my face
and it was dark, and I was clutching at an empty cloak,
and salt of my tears mingled with its salt);

I think I thanked my cousin for he broke an apple,
I always thought this was a clever trick
when we were children;

I think he smiled,
remembering my past effort and defeat;
"Lizeth," he said, "drink your red wine, eat this."

XVII

Lizeth? was Lizeth, Lilith in the Tree?
anger had drawn me back and out of time,
but now, I see in-time and passionately;

I would recall the symbols, name the Powers,
invoke the Angels, Tetragrammaton;
I am far from her now, but she is near,

chalking her circle with its letters on the attic floor;
step in it, Lizeth, dare Elizabeth Dyer,
to ponder on the secrets, writ in fire,

in the old book you found in the oak chest;
"our uncle's book," the cousin said and laughed,
"for this, he was disgraced," and read a list

of names, "exciting stuff—
let's call up Lucifer—do you remember how
we ran away and hid here, long ago?"

XVIII

He dragged me through the hedge,
"you used to laugh," he said, "Lizeth,
laugh and forget, be glad";

he kissed my face, "my flower, you are too pale,
I'll get you eglantine and the red pinks,
that we called sops-in-wine—do you remember?"

a bird whistled and a bird replied,
"so you see, everywhere, two and two, he said
"under the blossoming trees, the chestnut-spire,

the pear, you must have missed the garden,
that long year, London was always drear";
he drew me down beside him on the grass,

and he unfastened shoulder clasp and band,
and cupped my breasts within his firm young hands,
"so here" he said, "are peonies—and here—no rose is half so dear."

XIX

Could I forget, would I forget?
Lucifer, you have queens about you now,
Helen and Guinevere; Semiramis

orders her servants to direct the prow
toward Egypt—is it Egypt?
I will know tonight, when I escape

and stand within my circle; I marked it out
at first, but now it is invisible,
though its letters, copied from my uncle's book,

shine in the darkness, to invoke the Sephirs;
I would espouse your cause and find it good,
for I have understood at last,

the hints and pauses of you visitors,
the sudden turn the talk takes
whenever I appear, but shameless or inspired,

I hear, waiting a moment by the open door,
"he had strange traffic with daemonic powers,"
they said, "and spirits of the dead."

XX

His was not lover's talk, like Hugh's,
only the long, long stare by day,
with curtains drawn, or in the firelit dusk,
or by the candles, on the dressing table;

he flung his hat and cloak upon a chair,
and paced the length of the small room
and turned and always said, "I must go soon";
the room was not so small, it was the bed,

with crimson covers, an old bed from home
that took the space, but still there were
those narrow corridors, one at the foot,
one between bed and window, one by the door;

so he paced the floor, around, across, across,
around and back, until I fell,
driven as by a prowling lion or panther,
upon the crimson cover of the bed.

XXI

When Hugh's away at sea, I climb the stair,
the triangles and hexagons have grown dim;
the pentagon, the circle and the cross

have disappeared, but they are all inscribed
within my heart, the Tree of Life or Trees,
the pathways and the planets with their signs;

I can follow on from Mars to Venus,
to Jupiter, to Saturn, to the Crown, *Kether*,
and down again past *Daath*, past Mercury

to the core and root, *Malkuth*,
and on past the Dark Queen upon the throne,
Beth is her name or letter, after *Aleph*,

the priest or the magician by the altar;
there are the old prints in my uncle's book,
but I need not consult them any more;

I know one of the Trees is Rigor, one is Mercy,
and in between the two, the Tree of balance, equilibrium
leads on to Beauty, *Tiphereth*, the Sun.

XXII

For all the thrones and letters spell one story,
and only one, Love is the altar that we burn upon;

did he find that, after his frantic quest,
experiments, his journeys and the search

everywhere in old books, Latin and Hebrew texts?
Hugh helped when he was here, he told me how

they kept a sanctum in his house, above the river,
with astrolabe and crucible and a group,

dedicated to a secret cult of Night;
we talked of this and of our uncle's alchemy

and his disgrace; "find out for me what it was all about,"
I asked my cousin with false negligence,

"I want to know, I'll put away the book,
I promise not to read it any more,

or only now and then, consult it for a name
that comes and goes, not quite remembered,

and not quite forgot" (I laughed)
"that I must exorcise."

XXIII

"Now, tell me everything, Hugh, everything,"
"no woman should explore these devious rites,
no girl like you";

"our uncle blessed me with the angels' names
I found them in the book and now its clear,
he watches over us, he knows—"

"knows what?" "the Secret and the Sanctum,
how we met—I did not really know his name
till Agatha and Peter spoke of it,

after they took him; then I saw the part
he played in history, learned the plot;
you yourself spoke of this,

one night across the candles, at the table,
he honored his *parole,* you said—"
"my Lizeth, are you mad?"

"he came and went—you yourself said,
he bribed the gatekeepers, you yourself said,
he came and went, but never far—"

"but this was an impostor—" "no, no—for Peter knew him—"
"knew Sir Walter?" "O, do not speak the name,
perhaps another, an angel took his shape—"

"you mean a devil—" "but angels manifest sometimes
in forms of men—" "better it was Sir Walter
than your delirium of angels in men's forms."

XXIV

Tiphereth is beauty in that book,
the center and the Sun, an altar in the temple,
the shadow outline of an upright man;

can this be blasphemy? then what is beauty?
it is a square room and a bed within,
a square within a square, geometry,

the absolute answer to all alchemy;
he prowls along the narrow corridors,
at the foot, the bedside and the other side,

and as I lie waiting, I seem to see
myself, worshiping at the altar;
Semiramis, did I say, orders her servants

to direct the prow toward Egypt?
that was fantasy, but we are here;
this is Elizabeth Dyer,

we are in-time, today,
the past can neither add nor take away
from that small room, a square within a square.

XXV

The Tree, the Temple and the upright Man,
the square, the circle and add to the five,
the Oracle, my uncle's Seraphim;

he said the future would encompass us,
separate yet together, with their wings;
I do not need to seek their names,

their letters and their numbers in the book,
for they are ONE, yet doubled, two and two, a host
to sweep us to God's throne—and I am lost—

spare me myself, my small identity, I pray,
who should submit, soar higher, caught away;
spare me my name, Elizabeth, spare me his,

although he never said Lady Elizabeth,
nor I, Sir Walter—dear Lord,
do I remember now that time "before"—

for galleys crash and fire is flung,
and I again am standing on a wharf,
watching a tall mast slowly disappear.

XXVI

The past can neither add nor take away, I said,
but now "before" and "after" challenge each other,
a satrap or a monk with sunken eyes,

a memory of a purple sleeve, a memory of bliss,
a memory of repentance and slow death,
a memory of burning censors and the sulphur fumes

that vainly choke the half dead; there is hope;
there is no hope, the cart is at the door,
you can not sort them out; leave them

and nail them in, or take the lot?
whose is the voice, what executioner
condemns us all together?

XXVII

I am a ghost tending a little flame,
but one spark may ignite the host
of invisible Seraphim so that they

may visibly manifest on earth to men;
I speak his name, a thousand men appear,
or would if they could hear;

he could have ruled the realm, the world,
only he chose the way of love, Elizabeth (another, not the Queen)
and found himself (and with her) in the Tower;

that was his earlier plight, the later
was longer—I heard the story of his short release,
of his return, then of his death;

maybe my part was sheer delirium,
as Hugh once said; maybe, it was an angel
that paced the corridors about my bed;

maybe it was an angel in my room,
("my Lizeth—are you mad?")
or maybe as Hugh said, it was a devil.

XXVIII

It needed fire to generate remembrance,
Love was the *primum mobile,* the mediator,
Carthage, Rome, Tyre,

and on to the Cathedral's apse and nave
and the flesh crucified, until
remembrance brought us to this hour,

in which I strive, with or without
the litany and prayers, to save identity,
the Man—Angel or Devil.

XXIX

I do go back and clutch my precious book
and warm it at my breast,
it is the child I lost;

O infinite grace—my uncle granted me
this blessing and this peace,
here is a great sun, set between the trees

of Paradise, those same trees
with names of God, the same God
and yet other, some seventy names or more,

inscribed in the circumference of this Flower;
I dare not read them, printed on the page,
later, I'll light my candle, kneel and seek

the numbers and the names upon the chart,
divided round the circle of the year,
so one can find the special Angel

and God's special name
that guides the soul from birth;
I know his birthday and the day he died,

and my name on the chart lies not so far from his;
Azriel who saw him die, now let me live
to honor and to serve the names of God.

XXX

He honored his *parole* and loved,
and that has saved his soul and mine;

better the dim, sweet sanctuary of my room
and ignorance (mine) of his activity

with crucibles and astrolabes, of which they spoke,
his traffic with daemonic powers and spirits of the dead;

Lilith and Lucifer—let them not be lost,
O God of more than seventy names

and attributes of justice—let us keep these,
as symbols of our meeting, for his death

redeemed us, spared us, made the memory
of a little room, one of the aspects of eternity,

one of the stations, measured in that Sun
by rays from the circumference,

with numbers that again are found
in Paradise, upon the leaves;

we were one number; separate, we are two
upon the Tree of Heaven, *Sephirothique*.

XXXI

Julius come back, Julius come back,
I flamed too high and now I toss with fever,

there was a purple tent, there was a river,
there was real terror of barbaric hosts,

physical fear, but there was the escape,
the cup within my reach; even as you turned

to speak, before you parted the tent folds,
you said, "keep the wine till the last," and *vale,*

and paused with the fold lifted like a banner,
to add *ave* and dropped the folds and went;

the names I whispered on my knees,
the prayers I sent to heaven had no place there;

the world has punished us enough,
peace, peace, there was no Tower, no severed head,

peace, peace, there was no plague, penance, redemption,
but only at the last, your voice that said *ave.*

XXXII

"You can not beat them back, the garrisons are weak,
stay here, let Julia rest here in the garden,

Rome is doomed anyway, enjoy today today,
you are not Caesar, our great ancestor;

they won't get here tomorrow or next year,
or the year after, the legions are on guard about the walls,

there is enough to do here in the city,
see, Julia begs you stay," and Hermas put his arm

about my shoulder, "you almost disappear
among the lilies, in this white and silver";

O Hermas, comforter, you would have kept me there,
but I must disappear, though not among your lilies;

"a hunting trip? you can't get past the gates—"
"Octavius will help"—"Julia, you're mad"—

it was a simple matter after all,
and all discretion for the laticlave.

XXXIII

It was cool even amidst the furor,
our tent was set apart, with Octavius

always near to sound the alert
and help him with his armor;

within my thought, I prayed the Dioscuri,
no marble set in Hermas' corridor,

but beings in reality and near;
give us a Ship, we'll sail down this wide river,

the sea is not so far, I would forget
anxiety and ceaseless threat and war,

for we would found a City, greater
and with more power, even than ancient Rome.

XXXIV

No god set in an alcove, no god upon a plinth,
no plain Adonis, no slain Hyacinth,

for none slays Love, inconsequent and unpredictable,
he comes—how, no man knows,

and all the rest is leveled to the ground,
the city walls, the fortress and the Tower;

we stand alone, Julius and Julia,
the past, the future and the present, one;

what if we meet and do not know each other?
we'll meet again—we talked philosophy, Lucretius, Plato;

what if we meet, and one has gone the right,
the other on the lefthand path?

so we discussed the Eastern mysteries,
Pythagoras and rebirth; how often have we met like this,

how often have we separated, torn apart
in hate, bitterness and in disgrace?

XXXV

Ave and *vale,* but the parting came
before the greeting, it was *vale, ave,*

keep the wine till the last,
I hold this cup, I need not taste this sleep,

I hold the globe, as once so long ago
(or once, some centuries later),

I clutched the apple in my helpless hands
and could not break it—who would break this sphere,

this perfect crystal of reflected rose and red
and purple of the sanctuary, the tent folds,

or long ago (or was it centuries later?)
the crimson cover of an ark, a bed,

Sanctum Sanctorum where a stranger lay,
who always flung his cloak upon a chair,

and paced the room in urgency and fever,
and always said, "I must go soon."

XXXVI

The best wine came last, as we learnt long ago,
(or was it centuries later?) at the marriage feast;

the best will come, I know, when I drink this,
who knows, my Lord, how long before we meet?

What claims you now? do you instruct
new legions, do you plan a sudden sortie

on the race of man, and on the peril
of the man-made meteors?

would you destroy the whole to build again
the radiant city where man walks with man,

in confidence, invoking the benign
Omnipotence, who yet explains the pattern,

so we see even the smallest act,
in its proportion and significance;

but no—stay as you are a little longer,
stay as you are for years, for centuries,

and give me time to reinvoke the past
and read the future in this gazing glass,

this crystal of reflected rose and red,
for the best wine came last.

XXXVII

Now there are gold reflections on the water,
how old am I and how have the years passed?

I do not know your age nor mine, nor when you died,
I only know your stark, hypnotic eyes

are different and other eyes meet mine, amber and fire,
in the changed content of the gazing glass;

O, I am old, old, old and my cold hand
clutches my shawl about my shivering shoulders,

I have no power against this bitter cold,
this weakness and this trembling, I am old;

who am I, why do I wait here, what have I lost?
nothing or everything but I gain this,

an image in the sacred lotus pool,
a hand that hesitates to break

the lily from the lily stalk and spoil
what may be vision of a Pharaoh's face.

XXXVIII

"She is not grown, my Lord, a child
and without grace," an arm about my shoulder,

a voice—a gardner or a temple servant (Hermas?),
a dark, ironic face, a gesture and a glance,

the sound of metal on the marble pavement,
the bronze-edged sandal of a charioteer?

a soldier, captain or mere household-keeper,
one of the Pharaoh's men but not the Pharaoh,

one of the palace guard, not greater
than my protector, scribe and foster-father;

"later, my Lord, review the temple dancers
with me, there are new girls from Cos

and overseas, brought back since you last left;
my Lord, I am your servant,

and your campaign," he bowed,
"we learn, was most felicitous."

XXXIX

Then or much later, then or earlier,
then when time paused, for even time must pause

at a command—whose?—neither god nor Pharaoh
can subdue his stride, can laugh at time, the tyrant

and his scythe; reap armies, populations, whet your scimitar,
begin again on hoplites and the legions, even Alexander

stops at the horizon, but not we; there is a brazier
in a corridor, there is a blue cloth slung across a door,

there is the sound of curtain rings along the rod,
that then slide back and the blue curtain falls in its old folds,

and we are standing on a mosaic floor,
whose pattern is familiar, fish in water,

birds in the reeds, and a papyrus scroll
hangs on the wall; I see them there forever,

nor need turn and read the inscription
and translate the letters—for he can not read—

no business of a soldier—call a scribe—
but there are other symbols which he knows and sees,

and turns to appraise—one purple lily
in an alabaster vase.

XL

If there is urgency, there is no fear,
hail, yes, but not farewell,

Amenti flowered long before Eden's tree;
his hand invites the *delta* underneath

the half-transparent folds of the soft pleats,
and does not tear but draws the veil aside,

then both his hands grasp my bare thighs,
and clutch and tighten, bird claws or a beast

that would tear open, tear apart, but keep
the appetite at bay, to gratify a greater hunger

or to anticipate deeper enjoyment;
yet his commanding knees keep my knees locked,

even while his virility soothes and quickens,
till in agony, my own hands clutch and tear,

and my lips part, as he releases me,
and my famished mouth opens

and knows his hunger and his power;
and this is the achievement and we know the answer

to ritual and to all philosophy,
in the appeasement of the ravished flower.

XLI

I must have married Hugh: the house belongs to me,
the fields, the little river; visitors come and go,

even the Lady Abbess, a niece or daughter
of an old friend of my mother;

she is aristocratic and at ease but always says,
"Lady Elizabeth belongs to us;

she would have more leisure and more peace
at our Retreat," and she begs me come

not far across the fields, to Matins or Compline;
I smile apology and I decline,

remembering the old days and the old loyalties;
she does not know how once and feverishly,

I read my Missal till the pages faded
and the *Aves* cried, "it is another *Ave* that you seek,

a prayer within a prayer,
let life not spoil the hope of Paradise."

XLII

O, that was long ago, the purple lily,
and that was long ago, the *vale, ave,*

and that was long, long after, but the same
hunger, the same desire, the same appeasement,

in London, near the Tower, "my Lizeth, are you mad?"
for years, I faced Sir Hugh across the table,

after his father's death, for years, I spoke with gentlefolk
and kind, Hugh's cousins and our neighbors,

for years, I said, "when Hugh comes back,"
wearing the gowns he chose; a visitor

would look askance at Lady Elizabeth,
the ancient in her outmoded dress,

even although they had prepared the stranger,
"her husband's death—the shock—his ship *Seaspray*

was lost—you won't remember—off the coast
of Portugal, I think it was—long ago, James was king,

she's old—Oh very old—she can't remember
what happened yesterday . . ."

XLIII

What happened yesterday? a way of living,
a way of plunging reckless through the fires,

a way of waiting, "O, they'll soon pass over,"
a way of thinking, "where is Phoebe, do you think, Amico,

that one was nearer us or nearer her?
we might have sent her overseas—

if anything should happen—"
the doorbell or the telephone? "O, its you,

we were just wondering—" "it's all right,
the all-clear's sounded somewhere."

XLIV

What happened yesterday? a field of thorns,
grasp them, they turn to lilies,

the doorbell or the telephone? "O, do come in,"
he flung his hat and coat upon a chair,

it seemed we were familiar, *semblables,*
we were "familiars" and total strangers,

his eyes stared as his eyes had stared before,
nothing was changed, where everything was different,

the eagles and the legions, death and war,
the bronze-edged sandal of a charioteer,

London as always, it was just the same,
the coast guards and the signals and the fire.

XLV

There was no time to dream till it was over,
hail and farewell; there was no time

in which to read the pictures,
the message and the writing on the wall,

true, I transcribed the scroll,
he said he could not read—

no business of a soldier—call a scribe—
I did not know that he was more and further

than I could ever see—I did not know
that he knew everything, yet waited for an answer

in Egypt, in a sort of trance,
of patience and of fury, Oedipus, the King;

I gave the answer though I played the part
of prophetess or Sphinx, unknowingly,

I did not know he was invisible,
like Gyges with the ring.

XLVI

It took a long time to decipher this,
the Mystery, the Writing and the Scroll,

infinity portrayed in simple things,
in courteous answer or abrupt reply,

I read the surface script, it was enough,
no hat, no coat, but gloves flung on a chair,

"I wonder if I left my car in order,"
and he was off, down the three flights of stairs

and back, I waited for him at the door;
"I have less than an hour," he said,

and laid his watch beside him on the table;
he said, “I must rush off to meet my daughter”;

What did I know? I poured the tea,
I offered cigarettes, “no, no,” and he took up his watch

“now I must go,” and this was one of seven short visits
to decipher, seven meetings to decode.

XLVII

I transcribed the scroll, I wrote it out
and then I wrote it over, a palimpsest of course,

but it came clear, at last, I had the answer
or the seven answers to the seven riddles,

the why and why and why—the meetings and the parting
and his anger—it took some time, though five years is not long

to write a story, set in eternity but lived in—England;
I left of course; I traveled to the Tessin from Lausanne,

to Zürich and around and back again,
and I wrote furiously; he got the last of this prose Trilogy,

this record, set in time or fancy-dressed in history,
five years ago, then I had five years left

to break all barriers, to surpass myself
with *Helen and Achilles* . . .

an epic poem? unquestionably that,
I would not trouble him to read the script.

XLVIII

But bitterness sets in, a different sort of bitterness
but the same, the fear of fear that runs within my veins,

the fear of helplessness, of being lost;
O, I have many friends, Phoebe is safe,

I have three grandchildren; O, I have hosts
of friends—letters—the post? there's no anxiety,

is that the catch? let them lie there until I finish this,
I need not run them through, America, Italy, even a German stamp,

England of course; I need not fear to find or not to find
the envelope with the somewhat cramped address

and my name and the postmark not the same, not London now
but somewhere in the country;

O, that was long ago, the fire, the frenzy
and the Egyptian lily—

then let it go at that, he's safe, children, grandchildren
and a second wife.

XLIX

I wrote of course, congratulations and felicity,
a friend sent me the notice from a London paper,

Bridegroom of the Week, with the picture,
she smiled under a festive little hat,

her age? outside the official registrar;
the caption said, she wore sage green, was widow of one

of his former pilots, with a son,
how very suitable; he wrote a letter,

thanking me for mine, it was near Christmas,
and he enclosed the Christmas card from Lord-and-Lady,

and I sent back my card, addressed to both,
it was five years ago, and that was that.

L

It is not over, it has just begun; I read somewhere
in French I can't remember, only the word *semblables,*

that these "familiars" have the power of life and death
over each other; I think if I thought anything,

that I could help most with detachment and serenity,
"O, just keep out of it," I said when Christmas came,

and I could send a greeting with a Crown and Star,
something abstract, no angels at the manger,

O, wholly formal and in perfect taste,
and this made looking for my Christmas cards a game,

but no, I knew that I would never write,
"I'll never write again."

LI

I waited sixteen weeks and I was good,
at least, I think I was, "patience," they said,

"more patience" and "*Geduld*" they said, and Schwester Trude said,
"God wanted this, so you could have a rest";

I waited sixteen weeks and then was free, I thought,
"but at your age," they said, "the bone won't set,

you must go back to bed"; I said, "I'll try rebellion,"
for my prayers, I felt had failed;

I thought of you and then another picture came,
and article, Amico sent, "the usual thing," she wrote,

"the *au-delà* by your friend," and she enclosed
the cutting from the *Sunday Times,* your picture

and your comment on the other lives, Hell, Paradise,
and your pilots who were dead;

your friend? We've hardly named you through the years,
but you were there—and here—for suddenly,

I forged another prayer, hear me, O Master of the Air,
I cried, Light-bearer, pre-Adamic, Lucifer.

LII

Leave her, Elizabeth Dyer, the stage, the center,
she could walk, she could climb the attic stair,

could pray after a fashion, for a while anyway,
could invoke the past, could pore over the ancient books,

half guilty, half prophetic and half mad,
could believe in infinity and remember

how once her lover left the cup of sleep,
of death and of oblivion, within reach;

leave her, she can dream better than we,
remembering Sir Walter, she can see

further than we can see, can conjure up,
invoke, entreat, implore

the outline of an alabaster jar
and an Egyptian lily.

LIII

My friend, the river Thames ran past the door,
or not so far; barges and pageants now, for that was long ago,

the threat from Spain or somewhere else, the fire
that charred the warehouse and the priceless merchants' store

along the lower river; it ran a silver ribbon in the night,
you can't disguise the river, put out the light,

torch, lantern, brazier, lamp; crowd indoors by a candle,
you fortunate ones who can afford a candle;

wait, for your hour has come, O sinful city,
with a heretic upon the Throne, wait, for no watchman calls,

no voice is heard, and then the watchman woke
and the Lord God proclaimed, "your fate is in the balance,"

and the scales quivered and the seven weights showed
three one side, four the other, and the dark angels fell,

and the Apocalypse was clear to read,
not then in din and furor, but long after.

LIV

I mix my metaphors and history, my friend,
"I do not care for modern poetry," you wrote,

"I do not care for music or astrology"—why tell me that?
"I do not care for ceremonial"—and you gave a list,

all wrong, of what you called the rays, well, not wrong,
but illiterate or uninformed, the ray of healing

and the mental ray, I quite forget, but the impression
that you meant to give, remains, as of an amateur

dabbling in psychic matters, seriously but as recreation,
do you see? you left the way open for discussion,

could you trap me, you would trap me,
but we trapped each other, it was a serious matter,

Circe—
Gyges . . .

LV

And what had I? the common courtesies of a wrecked world,
"another cup of tea—a cigarette?" "no, no—do you mind this?"

and he pulled out his pipe, "of course, not—smoke,"
he did not stuff tobacco in the bowl, he lounged in the big chair

and nursed his pipe, and all confusion vanished, it was home,
he could call up enchantment and enchanters, the hero
of the moment

and all time, he was invisible but he was there;
I let the telephone ring on, ring on, I need not answer,

"but possibly, perhaps it is for you?" "no, no,"
nothing could spoil this moment, what we said

was immaterial, but we had to talk of something,
for the silence spoke of threat now past,

of the incalculable moment, when tense and resolute,
he flung the weight of "England's treasure," as he wrote of it,

into the balance and the balance swayed and hesitated,
and his heroic wings held and his wings beat back

the enemy, and in the silence there was all of this,
and of his thousand English pilots dead.

LVI

I am ashamed to speak of my predicament—
how long a prisoner? I who am so free,

my plight is nothing, I am fortunate;
"with bones like yours," the doctor said,

"so elegant, you can't expect a sudden miracle";
he did not say, "at seventy, it takes forever for a bone to heal";

and then there came the thought beyond the fear,
maybe there'll be a miracle, after all;

and then there came as answer to a prayer,
the thought, "maybe, I'll write a letter,"

I could simply say that I had read his article
and I could ask what else he'd written lately,

perhaps he'd like to hear, to know another
who'd traveled the same path, and got so far;

as far as what, as where? an armchair in a room,
a bed, a table, six months in Purgatory, no, not that,

five months perhaps, then this month, April,
with a breath from Paradise, when I seized my pencil

and my pencil wrote of the enchantment and the purple tent
        and how
following inexorable destiny, we met.

LVII

A sort of brusqueness and no nonsense,
but he liked the story; it was a game we played around a table,

Amico, a young Indian and his English mother;
I wrote of it after I heard him lecture and he wrote back,

it was the war of course and threat of death
that opened doors into this spirit-life;

I crowded with the rest to hear him speak,
he spoke casually, but it seemed sincerely;

our Indian friend had given me the ticket;
I squeezed in at the very last and thought,

how strange it was to hear him publicly,
speaking of messages and ghosts and spirits.

LVIII

The great days of the war had gone, we waited on,
he had retired; we had survived

the Battle and the threat of the invasion;
he seemed kind, fatherly and professorial;

one thought, he's not really talking down to us, an audience
who has faced annihilation with a joke

and cups of tea, common-or-garden English heroism,
girls in uniform and girls without, and older women,

rapt in ecstasy to hear the great and simple man
hold forth, talk to us in an easy friendly manner,

of people who were "here" and "there" as one,
stories and anecdotes, the sea, the Russian snow,

reports, he stated, given him by others,
automatic writers, mediums, extraneous matters,

no mention, it seemed odd, of his own men,
the part they played "before," what happened to them "after."

LIX

Our ancient vows—I lie alone—and everything is over—
no, not over, just begun—and if I think of Hugh,

it is the earlier England, I remember; I am forced
to think of things "before," in contrast to the "after,"

the venom and the anger, as of a Dragon standing guard
before a door—and I remember Hugh and how Sir Walter,

they said, had contact with daemonic powers and Spirits
        of the dead,
and this in only my comparison, who would accuse

the Master of the Air, the Air Marshal
who opened doors for many and for me—

and flung his hat and coat upon a chair,
and paced the floor and turned on me in fury . . .

and so remembrance brings us to this hour
in which I strive to save identity,

the Man—Angel or Devil—the *primum mobile,*
the mediator, destroyer and creator.

LX

And he was right and Hugh was right, "no woman
should explore these devious rites," how could I know

that he was Gyges and invisible, how could I know
that I was Circe with a secret key

and when the door swung open and was closed
swiftly, and he turned, the Dragon on the threshold,

in his fury, how could I know his fury was to save me,
that his repudiation was salvation.

LXI

Now you are old and tired and valiant, seventy-five a few days ago,
I wrote you for your birthday, once or twice,

for actually, I only knew you that one year,
though I had found you earlier through your lectures,

and we wrote and I sent messages from our Indian friend
and cards at Christmas and so on;

I followed out the guidance of *Alli,* so we called him,
or so he called himself or so his "guide," he said, had called him;

I find this is one of the over-seventy names of God,
seventy-two in fact, of which Elizabeth spoke;

I found her book in Lausanne on a shelf,
devoted to occult books, mostly French.

LXII

So I found your God-name or Elizabeth Dyer found it,
and your degree, thinking of your birthday,

Alla oddly, *Dieu adorable,* and mine not far
from yours, *Dieu qui inspire,* and *Teli,*

and there is *Alli, Dieu qui vivifie toute chose,*
your letters that he "read" me in the dark,

not knowing who had written them, not taking them
 from their envelopes,
with eyes closed, clairvoyantly seeing what the future held,

and "work" we had together, and some talk
of "a head off in the past," and of a monk

and of a being marked for some great destiny,
but longing for retirement and a time for contemplation
 and—a Ship;

the Ship was what inspired us, what brought *Alla* and *Teli*
to the ultimate goal of their ambitions and their hopes,

for it had come over and above the stresses and the fury
 and the fear,
bearing its priceless treasure,

"O, so many," Alli said, "shouting and laughing";
the Ship was for you.

LXIII

I like to think, to make the almost unbearable story bearable,
that Hugh was there, I like to think that the *Seaspray* returned,

with other phantom ships, to hail them as they fell,
and gather them together on that one mysterious Ship

that brought *Alla* and *Teli* together, that the miracle
extended through all time, but that eternity

was not a vast conception of philosophy,
but a simple plane, a near extension of our own common time,

where clocks tick and where no evil forces
shatter the continuity of your lives,

and where courtesy controls humanity,
and where the Master of the Air

says simply, "pride failed—
but all through time, I waited for you."

LXIV

Now will you laugh, my friend, I mean a cigarette,
this *near extension of our own common time,*

and chestnut spires, so lovely in the dusk,
I saw them and I breathed their anodyne,

but they come and close the window when the light is on,
for the *Maikäfer* bumps and zooms about my bed,

and he is hard to catch and the night-sister says,
"you can't have both, the open window and your table light";

so now I tell you this and now I'll reach
for cigarette and match, and this will be

my high philosophy (I know you'll understand),
remembrance of the seven times we met.

LXVI

I should be too old for exaltation,
I am too old, but inexplicably,

spring threatens with enchantment
and I almost fear redemption through its beauty:

doors open, one door shut inexorably,
but I had sensed the depth and I was spared;

I traveled, I was happy, even although
the path had led from darkness

on through darkness, back to illumination,
and from illumination, to despair,

and from despair to inspiration,
and as answer to a prayer,

the *VALE AVE* and the thought beyond the fear,
perhaps there'll be a miracle, after all.

LXV

How could anything so complicated be so simple,
how could anything so difficult be so clear?

I mean "the cloud of witnesses" that worried us
as children and the Holy Ghost?

but strangely, it couldn't have happened, not to us,
without the good and bad of our predicament,

without Elizabeth, a sort of Marguerite to your Faust,
without the undercurrent that just didn't wreck us,

an invisible Circe or disguised Lilith,
or Helen, Guinevere, Semiramis,

that we invoke as Graces, even Virtues,
not for their beauty only, but for their implacable search

for the *semblable,* the haunting first cause,
the *primum mobile* that gave both Hell and Paradise to Dante;

perhaps, I boast, perhaps I should be cowed and disciplined,
a woman of seventy, lying—no—not helpless,

for I called for light,
and *Dieu qui inspire,* Light came.

LXVIII

He might have been an ancient Cabalist,
none other than Ezra-Azriel returned, or another,

or many others, Socrates, of course;
O, he was sly and secret and revealed infinite secrets,

but the secrets kept were greater
than we dreamed of or dared dream;

I once apologized, "you must not think me superstitious,
but you seventy-seven" I said, "is eloquent;

I mean the number in itself"—and waited,
but he did not answer, he just let it go;

and once I had a dream-sequence of Houses and I said,
"I think its astrological, a friend in England

sends me star charts and maps; this is outside
our work, I know; I mention it only

because of the dream-sequence and the association
with your Star, Venus"; then he seemed to start

as if suddenly discovered and off guard, and said
with a sort of ironical amusement and half worship, "not *Venus*."

LXIX

Why do these words seem suddenly to laugh?
Onkelos, Hebrew?

or maybe it isn't Hebrew; I read of the *Targum de Jérusalem.*
attributed to *Onkelos*—is *Onkelos* Greek? no matter,

it is a question of *traditions transmises par la parole*
and "Parole" is in Hebrew, *Kabalah,* and in French, *Kabal;*

so he honored his *parole,* I said,
meaning his personal word, his honor,

and maybe, there were other vows, impersonal, hieratic,
including whole cycles of lodges, Houses, *cénacles,*

and an oath is sacred, and the punishment, I read,
for revealing initiation secrets, may be death;

how could I laugh at this? I do not laugh—
witness, O Father, *Dieu, père secourable.*

LXX

I am frightened, I confess, to write of this,
and yet I flaunt the adventure, bear the secret

like a banner; I even laugh, or rather as I said,
the words laugh, though I added (slightly shivering,

following my pencil, slightly alarmed, wondering what would
follow),
how could I laugh at this?

but there is laughter somewhere, far off at sea,
unconquerable, gay, heroic, unheard by us

but conveyed to us by *Alli,* and another sort of laughter,
sly, discreet and near, of another unconquered Spirit,

the Star of our Father, whose God-name, I find
is *Zaka* and whose attribute, *Dieu, père secourable.*

LXXI

He wrote in the end, that the messages were "frivolous,"
so Nemesis woke or Fate, symbolically wearing the crown

of metal spear points from the shattered lance staves,
a crown to be worn proudly, not easily set aside,

and a dark mourning robe over the fragile stuff,
the pleated linen hidden, the transparencies, semitransparencies

of the bride; yet even these words are inadequate,
for what happened, happened, it was a tour-de-force,

a trick of the hermetic "Joker" of the old alchemists,
no need to wonder why or how, or invoke Nemesis.

LXXII

Now there is only laughter, "O, so many," *Alli* said,
"shouting and laughing, and a name *Teli,*

Dieu qui inspire, and a bride; there is only now
and the hereafter, antithetical perhaps, but running side by side,

body and soul, spirit and body, the old problem,
the old pattern, complicated, simplified, translated and decoded,

Athens, Alexandria, Carthage, Rome, Freud—
he would have understood, followed the story

with admiration, sympathy, perhaps concern
lest I fall victim to abstract speculation,

or fall a victim to the Air Lord and his pride,
he would have felt the threat and the temptation,

he must have followed us, standing aside,
he must have hailed the Ship

that brought the messages, "Parole," the Word,
and added his breath to the breath of God.

LXXIII

Light follows darkness, and the darkness light,
the Dragon-lover of mythology was not chained in the pit,

Hannibal, Caesar, Martel,
but ploughed the earth inexorably,

and the sea, and last the *Dragon volant* sought the sky,
to inaugurate a new age and a new mythology,

a new Circe, Helen, Lilith;
what she sees, Helen, Semiramis, *Teli,*

is at best inadequate, fragmentary, but she saw *Alla,*
a whole, complete, armed for the divine event,

and unarmed when venomous before the threshold,
he turned to attack her, crowned.

LXXIV

There is *Alla, Teli* and our Indian friend, *Alli,*
there is *Zaka* unquestionably, and Amico

who sent me your last picture, is *Dieh,*
with the attribute, *Dieu qui délivrez des Maux,*

there are all the others, on earth, a "cloud of witnesses,"
as in heaven; may these deliver us

from all iniquity, questioning and distrust,
and at the last (I know they'll understand),

I ask for this, the blessing of the Ship, of the "Parole,"
in remembrance of the seven times we met.

A KNIFE ALL BLADE

or: usefulness of fixed ideas

JOÃO CABRAL DE MELO NETO

Translated from the Spanish by Kerry Shawn Keys

TRANSLATOR'S NOTE: *João Cabral de Melo Neto (1920–) is Brazil's best-known post-World War II poet. He has published continuously since 1942:* Pedra do Sono (Sleep Stone), *1942;* O Engenheiro (The Engineer), *1945;* Fábula de Anfion *and* Antiode (The Fable of Anfion *and* Anti-Ode), *1947;* Psicologia da Composição (The Psychology of Composition), *1947;* O Cão sem Plumas *and* O Rio (Featherless Dog *and* The River), *1954;* Os Três Mal-Amados (The Three Loveless Men), *1954;* Paisagens com Figuras, Uma Faca só Lâmina (Landscapes with Figures *and* A Knife All Blade), *and* Morte e Vida Severina (Severine Life and Death), *1956;* Quaderna (*1960*); Dois Parlamentos (Two Speeches), *1960;* Serial (*1961*); A Educação pela Pedra (Education through Stone), *1966; and* Museu de Tudo (Museum of Everything), *1975.*

In terms of technique, Cabral has developed a dry, ascetic diction that avoids metaphorical language and other traditional poetic devices, relying instead on simple, stark vocabulary and an absolute economy of expression. Thematically, Cabral's poetry has evolved along two complementary lines that many critics have seen as expressing opposing epistemologies, but which in reality express the same existential posture in different ways. One line of development focuses on the poet's native Pernambuco, an underdeveloped, desert state in the Brazilian northeast, similar to New Mexico or Arizona in its climate. In the poems with this tendency, the poet emphasizes poverty and deprivation, and critics have stressed the protest dimensions of this work to the exclusion of its philosophical message. (Poetry in this line would include Featherless Dog, The River, *and* Severine Life and Death, *for example.) The philosophical orientation of these poems, however, unites them with the other tendency, in which ontological and epistemological concerns predominate, and there is a sustained exploration of the contemporary meaning of aesthetics. Poems in this line include the poet's Spanish poems, such as* A Knife All Blade, *but there is a pervasive Spanish influence in the social poems as well.—KSK*

Just like a bullet
buried in the body,
pressing down one side
of the dead man:

just like a bullet
of heaviest lead
in the muscle of a man,
weighing him down on one side;

like a bullet with
its own firing power,
a bullet possessing
an active heart,

a heart like a clock
sunk deep in the body,
like a living clock
that always rebels,

a clock having
the cutting edge of a knife
and all the impiety
of a steel-blue blade;

just like a knife
without pocket or sheathe
transformed into part
of your anatomy,

an intimate knife,
a knife for internal use,
inhabiting the body
like the very skeleton

of the man who would have one,
and always, full of pain,
of the man who would wound himself
against his own bones.

A

Be it bullet, clock,
or furious blade,
it is nevertheless an absence
that such a man carries.

But what is not in him
is like a bullet:
it contains the iron of lead,
the same compact fiber.

What is not in him
is like a clock
beating in its cage,
without fatigue, without rest.

What is not in him
is like the jealous
presence of a knife,
of any unseasoned knife.

For this reason the best
of the symbols employed
is a cruel blade
(better if a Sheffield):

because nothing can indicate
this so ravenous absence
like the image of a knife
that would have only its blade,

because nothing indicates better
this greedy absence
than the image of a knife
reduced to its mouth,

than the image of a knife
entirely delivered
to hunger for those things
that are felt by knives.

B

Most astonishing
is the life of such a knife:
a knife or any metaphor
can be cultivated.

Even more astonishing yet
is its culture:
it doesn't grow from what it eats,
but rather from what it fasts.

You can abandon it,
that knife in the guts:
you will never find it
with an empty mouth.

From nothing it distills
acid and vinegar
and other tricks
peculiar to sabers.

And like the knife it is,
fervent and energetic,
without assistance it fires
its perverse mechanism:

the stript blade which grows
as it wears,
the less it sleeps
the less sleep there is,

the more it cuts
the sharper its edge
and it lives to produce itself
in others like a spring.

(For the life of such a knife
is measured in reverse:
be it clock or bullet,
or be it the knife itself).

C

Careful! with the object,
with the object be careful,
though it is only a bullet
studded with lead,

because the teeth of the bullet
are already quite blunt,
and quite easily become
more blunt in the muscle.

Take more care, however,
when it becomes a clock
with its heart
burning and spasmodic.

Pay special attention
so that the pulse of the clock
and the pulse of the blood
do not interlock,

and that its copper, so polished,
does not enmesh its pace
with blood that already beats
without a bite.

But if it is the knife,
O, be more careful:
the sheathe of the body
may absorb the steel.

Likewise, its edge, at times
tends to get hoarse
and there are cases in which blades
degenerate into leather.

Of grave importance is that the knife
not lose its passion
nor be corrupted
by its wooden haft.

D

And at times, this knife
turns itself off.
And that's what's called
the low tide of the knife.

Perhaps it isn't turned off,
perhaps it only sleeps.
If the image is a clock,
its bee ceases to buzz.

But whether asleep or turned off:
when such an engine stops,
the entire soul turns base
like an alkaloid,

quite similar to a neutral
substance like felt, which
composes the souls that lack
the sharp skeleton of a knife.

And the sword of this blade,
its flame flashing before,
and the nervous clock,
and the indigestible bullet,

all of them follow the process
of the blade that blinds:
they become knife, clock
or bullet of wood,

bullet of leather or cloth,
or a clock of pitch,
they become the knife without backbone,
the clay-knife, the honey-knife.

(Yet, when the tide
is no longer expected,
the knife suddenly resurges
with all its crystals.)

E

It is necessary to keep
the knife well hidden
because in dampness
its flash dies out

(in dampness created by
the spit of conversation,
the more intimate it is
the stickier it gets).

Caution is necessary
even if the live coal that
inhabits you isn't a knife,
but a clock or a bullet.

For they can't withstand
all climates:
their savage flesh
demands rough quarters.

But if you must expose them
in order to better bear them,
let it be in some barren plain
or wasteland in the open air.

Never remove them in air
occupied by birds.
It must be a harsh air,
without shade, without vertigo.

And never at night,
never in night's fertile hands.
Let it be in the acids
of the sun, in the torrid sun,

in the fever of this sun
that turns grass to wire,
that makes a sponge of the wind
and makes thirst out of earth.

F

Whether it be that bullet
or any other image,
even if a clock be
the wound that keeps,

or even a knife
that wants only its blade
(of all images, the most
voracious and graphic),

no one will be able
to remove it from his body
whether it be a bullet,
a clock, or a knife,

and the race of the blade
is also unimportant:
whether a tame table knife
or the ferocious bowie.

If he who suffers its rape
can't pull it out,
how could the hand
of a neighbor remove it.

The entire medicine
of arithmetical tweezers
and numerical knives
can do nothing against it.

Neither can the police
with all their surgeons,
nor can time itself
with all its bandages.

And neither can the hand
which, without knowledge,
planted the bullet, clock or knife,
images of fury.

G

This bullet that a man
carries at times in his flesh
makes him that keeps it
less rarefied.

And what this clock implies
for the impetuous and the insect
is that, when locked in the body,
it makes it more alert.

If the metaphor is a knife,
carried in the muscle,
knives inside a man
give him greater force.

The cutting edge of a knife
biting a man's body
arms his body
with another body or dagger,

for by keeping alive
all the springs of the soul
it provides the blade its attack,
and the bayonet, its sexual heat,

and, in addition, a body
coiled tightly on guard,
insoluble in sleep
and in everything empty,

as in that story
told by someone
of a man who fashioned
a memory so precise

that he could preserve
in his palm, for thirteen years,
the weight of a hand,
feminine, pressing.

H

When he who suffers words
labors with words, the clock,
the bullet, and especially
the knife are useful.

Men who generally
work in this business
keep only extinct words
in the warehouse:

some words suffocate
under the dust,
others go unnoticed
among the great knots;

words that lost in their use
all the metal and sand
that holds the attention
which wants to leave.

For only this knife
will give such a worker
eyes more fresh
for his vocabulary

and only this knife
and the example of its tooth
will teach him to obtain
from sick material

that quality which all knives
keep as their essence:
a ferocious acuteness,
a certain electricity,

plus the pure violence
that they have in such precision,
the taste of the desert,
the style of knives.

I

This hostile blade,
this clock, this bullet,
if it makes more alert
all those who guard it,

it also knows to wake
the objects around it,
even the very liquids
begin to grow bones.

For whoever suffers the knife,
all the sluggish matter,
all that was vague,
acquires nerves, edges.

Everything acquires
a more intense life—
the sharpness of a needle,
the presence of a wasp.

In each thing the side
that cuts reveals itself,
and they that looked
as round as wax

now strip themselves
from the callus of routine,
they set out to function
with all their corners.

Among so many things
that already can't sleep,
the man whom the knife cuts
and to whom it gives its edge,

suffering that blade
and its thrust so cold,
he passes, lucid and sleepless, he goes
cutting edge against cutting edge.

†

Back from that knife,
friend or enemy,
which compresses a man more
the more it chews him;

back from that knife
carried so secretly,
and which must be carried
like the hidden skeleton;

from the image where I stayed
the longest, that of the blade,
because of all the images
it is surely the most greedy;

once back from the knife
one ascends to the other image,
that of the clock
gnawing under the flesh,

and from it to the other,
the first, that of the bullet,
which has a thick tooth
but a strong bite,

and from there to the memory
that dressed such images
and is much more intense
than the power of language,

and at last to the presence
of reality, the first,
that which created memory
and still creates it, still,

at last to reality, the first,
and of such violence
that in trying to grasp it
every image splits.

A CIVIL CAMPAIGN

JULIA THACKER

Sex, at first, was not even considered. When they flew him home from Vietnam, the bullet still lodged in his spine, the doctors weren't sure he would live. Then the question was, "Would he walk?" He would not. Then, "Would he have bladder and bowel control?" He would not. Leah was afraid he wouldn't recognize her in his delirium, but before the last operation he opened his eyes, looked at her, and whispered, "On fire." Only since he had become fully conscious did he no longer seem to know her. Beyond polite answers, he seldom spoke. He lay there, a black, hulking mystery, like the god to whom she had tried to pray as a child. As an offering, she watered the philodendron in his ward. She believed the silences between them meant something.

With the disability checks she rented a first-floor apartment near the hospital, overlooking a city park. The resident psychiatrist said Gus should be made to feel useful, so she spread swatches of purple silk, denim, and white velvet on his bed in a ceremony of color and said, "Choose, choose." The man without hands in the next bed suggested a fake fur sofa for the living room. Gus said, "Whatever you think is fine."

The psychiatrist continued to speak to Gus's stony face about his "adjustment." He said the relationship with Leah would not be easy now, especially since they didn't yet know if Gus's injury resulted in impotence; but there were many ways to express love and affection. He gave Gus a book, *Sex for the Elderly*, with "useful information." In Physical Therapy Gus learned to lift himself from the wheelchair to the car, so Leah had only to fold the chair and put it in the back seat.

"You'll like the apartment," she said.

"I'm sure I will." Gus could not remember if it was Leah or a bar girl who said, "It tickles my nose, like wood burning." Perhaps it had been a nurse while he was sick. "Do you mind if I smoke?" he asked.

"No, please, go ahead."

That Leah might leave him was a possibility that occurred to neither of them. She had not even the address of her mother, somewhere in the South; Gus, no one else.

Gus knew her walk first. From the picture window of the bar where he was manager, he used to watch her step off the bus in her waitress uniform and disappear around the corner. It was a fast, proud walk with a model's twist, but somehow natural. Sometimes he stood in the doorway and called, "On fire!" She turned and smiled. One day he came out into the street and pulled her into the bar. "Why you late, Sunshine? You my watch, baby. I don't admit the birds awake till you walk down this street."

"Phone for Gus," someone yelled.

He gripped her hand, and they did a half-Watusi across the floor to Stevie Wonder. "Not bad," he laughed, "for a little white girl." She struggled free of him while he was speaking on the telephone.

"I'm already late now."

He clapped his hand over the mouthpiece, "Like, a, would it be ap-pro-pri-ate for me to call you sometime? You're really attractive. I'd really like to get into," he looked the length of her, "your head."

Usually they stayed in his room above the bar. She told at once how her mother had thrown her out of the house when she found out Leah was sleeping with her husband, Leah's stepfather.

"I guess he was somebody to care about," Leah said. "But all he wanted was *two* women in the house."

Gus held her hands above her head while they made love.

"I don't know if I ought to rape you or protect you."

"Which do you want to do?"

"I want to do both."

She circled him with her legs, drawing him nearer. He talked in time with his moves in and out of her.

"We gonna go to Paris, gonna go to Portugal . . . Forget about that daddy of yours, you got me now. He don't know your rhythms like I do, does he, baby? . . . We gonna get a Cadillac with diamond hubs." He went deeper into her. "You can be the moon too, tell me when to give up to Darkness, that old bastard. He the one been fucking with my baby." She got on top.

Their new Colonial brick apartment was framed by trees the unreal, deep hues of Indian summer.

"Can I fix you some dinner before I bring the things in from the car?" she asked, as they stepped in.

"Not hungry," he mumbled. Nor did he seem interested in the decor, the baskets of orange paper roses that filled the living room. "I hate to mention this," he said, "but could you help me in the bathroom with these plastic pants? I haven't got the hang of getting them on and off yet.

"Sure, come on." Leah pushed him into the bathroom and helped him off with his pants and a diaperish contraption. She could not quit staring at his familiar body, thinner now, and his limp cock, which, curiously, she expected to harden, grow magically. He had looked important and heroic in the hospital, the nurses and doctors ministering to him in their white gowns; but against her shower curtain, the plunger, her bottles of talcum and cologne, he was merely pitiful. She switched on the fluorescent lights, and Gus squinted against the glare. It was like the rockets at night, what he hated most in Nam. When in the bush, where there were no electric lights, he could wipe out everything in the black sky, until the rockets began their yellow designs, the noise of distance, reminding him who and where he was. He hated them because they were so beautiful, death's fireworks. He didn't want to die.

"You go out," he told Leah. "I can handle the rest of this." He shut the door, so she wouldn't see the way his hands shook, and turned out the light.

While Gus napped in the evening, Leah brought in his valise, then sat down at the table to make lists of things that would make him more comfortable, each new column with a different color felt-tipped pen: cantaloupes, avocados, berries, walnuts; games, colored pencils, magazines, records; handkerchiefs, coverlets; until she had surely thought of everything, freeing herself to fall upon the sofa-bed in blankness, where, later, she felt his shadow pass over her face.

"I can still eat you out," he said from the doorway, a toneless fact. "You used to like it."

"All right."

He turned his back while she stripped, removed his terrycloth robe and folded it neatly on a chair. As he came closer, she was sick from the stink of wet plastic. He touched her all over, his hands skillful as a watchmaker's. But she was someone else *I'll think of a black box within a black box* who didn't even recognize her own voice. He put two pillows under her, bending from the waist, and cupped her ass in his hands. When he brought his face down her foot brushed a chrome spoke on his chair, but he thought her cry was because of his tongue. He wanted to remember the last time with Leah, as a way of being true to her, yet he held only the image of a young girl who, one night when he was high, told him she was pregnant. "It could be anybody's," he told her. "When it's born you see," she insisted. "Oh, wonderful, what a mixture," he said, "nigger and slant-eyed cunt." He listened to Leah's moves and sighs as to a cello, and when they reached a certain pitch, he stopped and rolled into his room. Leah put on her gown and straightened the bedclothes, stuffing the sheet in her mouth to keep her crying from the bedroom, where he lay quietly.

There was an unspoken agreement (she supposed because she did not work the next day) that he would come to her on Tuesday and Saturday nights, fold his robe, and wait for her to strip. Their lives were a set score, a familiar record one puts on because he knows the lilts and crescendos and can listen without particularly feeling anything. They passed each other in the house with polite remarks, the music echoing of the walls in empty rooms.

Each day she rose at seven. In the bathroom she could hear Gus's clock radio as he did his twelve-minute barbell exercises. By the time he was ready to shave, she had applied her make-up and dressed. She laid out the lace tablecloth and napkins for coddled eggs and the Melba toast Gus liked. When he came in, the three newspapers she subscribed to were on the table, and they ate and read in silence. "Will you sit in the park today?" she would call from the door, and he would say he might.

One morning in late November there was an overnight frost and, because the landlord had not turned on the heat yet, Leah woke up early. She opened the curtains and stood in the sunlight to warm herself. She placed two logs in the fireplace and lit them, but still she could not stop shivering. The newspapers hadn't arrived; it was too early. On the front stoop there were only two bottles of milk, which Leah took into the kitchen. She decided to get ready for the diner and tried over and over again to draw a steady line under her eyes and around her lips, smudging every time. Gus was awake too, rumbling around, waiting to get into the bathroom, so she gave up and rinsed all color from her face. She set the plates on the table, started the percolator and toast. Gus wheeled in and sat fidgeting when he found there were pieces of ice in the bottle. When she shook it to release the liquid, Gus's glass overflowed on his hand.

"I'm so sorry," she said.

"Please, don't worry about it. It's all right."

She got the toast and coffee, and they began to eat, forced to look across at one another. Slowly, she saw her own strain mirrored in the rings under his eyes, the hollow cheeks, until she wanted to scream, wanted some noise to fill the vacant room and this man, just as hollow.

"Are you going out today or not?"

"I don't know," he said. "The park is always full of kids. They get on my nerves."

"Why don't you spin your wheels and scare them off?" Leah asked. Her voice rose. "Why don't you yell at them, throw breadcrumbs, anything to show you're still a man? I'd like to be there to see it." And she giggled in relief.

He rolled over to her. "You'll see it, bitch," he said, raising his hand to strike her, but the wheels locked, throwing him forward. It was not the arc he made in air, nor even that he did not put his hands out to break the fall which moved her to him; rather, it was that he said her name *Leah*. She sat cross-legged on the floor, running her hand over every part of his body in search of a bruise, a broken bone, or simply to confirm his presence, where he lay, one knee in the east and one in the west, his palm flat on her face. She unzipped his pants, pulling the layers of underthings to his knees.

"Make something happen to this dick," he said. Her mouth rose and fell, a soundless O. There were only the ticks of the clock, the dry wood popping, and his sighs, punctuated with her name *Le, Le, Le.* He came like a hole in the garden hose in her mouth, spilling the warmth down her throat and through her. Her face next to the carpet, she noticed a white spot.

"I'll have to move and get cleaned up," he said.

"Yes."

They tidied his clothes, and he gripped the table, as he would get into a car, to lift himself into the chair. As Leah pushed him into the bathroom, she touched the wheelchair, its sharkskin back, shiny, which held a kind of beauty for her now, because it belonged to them, it was intimate, like a sadness no one speaks of.

FOUR POEMS

ALLEN GROSSMAN

A LITTLE SLEEP

I

Lying on my right side, I see the wall.

Lying on my left side, I see the window.

Facing the wall, lying on my right side
(Easing the ache in my left arm), I see
As in a dream the same wall closer to
My eyes.

Facing the window (lying on my hurt
Left arm again), I see the garden beyond
The window, almost out of sight above
My eyes. Looking at the window, I am
Affronted by the opaque light concealing
Everything, except a few branches high up.

Turning once again onto the ache in
My right arm, I see the white wall flaking
To older red underneath,

and remember
The branches high up, now behind my back.

II
Facing the wall, my right hand reaches the
Bed's head, which is a dark high cloud of wood
Reticulated downward in windy scrolls,
And my right foot touches the bed's cold foot.

My right cheek lies, almost without sensation,
On the sheet.

By pressing with my left foot
Against the bed's foot, I can make the ache
Less in my right shoulder. But my erect
Penis (lying this way) is jammed between
My belly and the bed's grave underworld
To the point of pain.

The whole bed hangs cloudlike
Above the floor.

To my left is the wall
Like an erased Book of the Dead. To my
Right is a window high up, shallowest
Of eyes.

The bed's head is above my head,
And beneath my feet is the bed's cold foot.

III
The bed stands between the wall and window.

On the bed lies a shadowy boy who must
Be consoled,

and also a man who must
Believe the consolation, which should be
A sentence he can say that the boy can
Understand.

The boy is the man when young,
And I am the man now, remembering the
Branches high up, perhaps with wind in them.
There seems so much to say about the few
Branches,

which might be anywhere, in this
Or another time, seen through the affront
Of light by this man or boy,

lying in
The ache of his left side (weary of much
Turning) who remembers the visionary blank
White wall, flaking to red, so near his eyes.

IV

Turning to the window (my penis is
Easier now, but my right shoulder is cold)
I feel more like sleep.

Seeing the branches
High up in this or another time, the
Shadowy boy stares at the branches, his
Mouth swollen with hunger, his penis aching,
His right shoulder cold.

Lying on my left
Side my left hand reaches to warm my right
Shoulder, and my right hand holds my penis, or
(Very gently) the boy's. The light batters
The branches.

We sleep a little, and sleeping
The same branches appear with a steady wind
In them.

In my right hand his penis grows
Less troubled. Reaching my left hand into
The shadow under his left shoulder I warm
His right shoulder, together with my own.

I say nothing. A little sleep is good.

V

As I turn again onto my right side

The shadowy boy turns with me, pressing
His penis between my legs, and his pained
Mouth (very gently) against my neck.

Waking
Now I see before my eyes, on the erased
Death-page of the blank wall, the shadows of
The high branches which are behind my back,
In the inscribing light.

The ache in my
Right arm starts. The dream was like the waking,
After a little sleep.

My cold left shoulder
Warmed by my right hand, I face the shadowy
Blank white wall flaking to the older red,
Which was the color this room was before

I made it ready, and lay down to stare—

The bed's cold foot beneath my feet, and
Above my head the high bed's dark cloud head.

VI
Getting up (rising on my right elbow,
And twitching the blue quilt behind me with
My left hand, standing, etc.) is more complex
Than I can explain.

The garden appears,
Level to my eyes, with paths severely
Indicated by the light.

The dear shadow
Has vanished, or dispersed into the disturbed
Bed between the great head and the chill foot.
Now, you console him. Warm him in your arms
As I have done. Kiss his penis, and his
Pained mouth now addressed to you.

I can go
Either to the right, or left,

seeing or
Remembering the garden with branching
Paths, and the visionary page erased,
Or faintly inscribed

(White over red, shadow over the white)
By a strengthless, hasty, obsessive hand.

THE PROTHANATION OF A CHARIOTEER

David Zil'berman
(born Odessa, 1938—died Waltham, Mass., 1977)

La combat spirituel est aussi brutal que le bataille d'hommes; mais la vision de la justice est la plaisir de Dieu seul. Rimbaud

I
It was as if

something had slipped from me,
Down a sharp stair—;

as I waked from a short
Dirty sleep in a low chair

in August
Burdened with my dream of phantom Zil'berman
Dead at just this void time of year,

and now
Reposing

through his *jahrzeit*

in the frescoed
Chamber of a cheap coffin (The lid was
Cracked, and let in light), wearing a gay pair
Of striped pants bought for him in Chicago
By his wife,

in the Jewish cemetery
In Waltham, Massachusetts—near the fence . . .

Did this really happen?

Was David here?
A far cry from Odessa where he was born,
Or the high Turkman desert of Kara Kum
Where, as a Sanskrit weather man, he learned
That he,

perhaps alone of men, would finish
In happiness the work begun,

being the
Thirty-fourth incarnation of Śankara,
A Hindu sage, whose parents chose to have
One wonder son of merit who would live
To no great age;

but not (my God!) that he
Would have his skull crushed by an adolescent
In a stolen car

(The terms of spiritual combat are obscure.)

as he returned at
Evening on his bicycle, from an untimely
Seminar;—

And, having nothing in his pockets, die
Unidentified, and thus

be houseled by
A priest, buried a Jew,

and mourned a bitter
Husband, and a haunting friend (intimate
Alien with transparent hands),

the father
Of some girls

(quite absent-minded now), also
Mysterious philosopher, the one
Perhaps who *knew* . . .

II

And so it was as if
Something slipped from me irretrievably
Down a sharp stair to a phosphoric sea,
Waking me from my low chair—.

In humid August,
Drenched with Caspian air,

the unsown graveyard
Was scattered everywhere with tiny, yellow
Flowers, a sort of dust—

intricate, five-petaled,
Nameless, gay.

I raised a yellow flower to
My eye,
And all the petals fell away,

either because
The flower was wild, or else it was mid-
Afternoon, and late in the life of flowers
That live one day . . .

"There is no picture
Without an artist," David used to say,
"But the artist without a picture is
Divinely free."

I cannot hear the voice
Of holy Zil'berman. It had no tone.

And when he talked, he wandered around the room.

III
The graveyard is on the right of South
Street, as you go down from the University
Toward Main.

I used to see him walking home,
But on the left side,

as through a forest,
Or beside a sea,
With his hand on hip, head up, like a guide

Or, like a charioteer walking beside
A vast chariot with a high chair, and mere
Streak of galactic wheels, so real I could
Not see,

but with a sound that I could hear—

(Unless I only heard the roar of the
Boy in the fast car, coming on, that brushed
His handlebar, and made the catastrophe.)

O, who would believe that as a man dies
Who knows nothing, or very little, so also
Dies the sage?

(Where were the marks, then, summer weather man?—
The high stable illusions of your golden
Colchis, where the white carp in rows suck like
Pigs at the bland teat of the warm littoral;
And the mariners steer by the bright mirage,
Steadier than our stars?)

Specific chapters of certain
Books will now lament inconsolably—
They have lost their understander forever;
"The Structure of the Chariot," and also

"The Book of the Aśvattha" lift up un-
Intelligible voices

(Now they are
Men of tears).

The Modal Methodology—his
Pale mother, in her throes—has veiled her lips.
The tent has fallen of the Transcendental
Reduction, and weeps for David Zil'berman,
A man whole, with all his desires.

But the face
And the great eyes of Gregory Palamas
Signify, "Let there be silence. . . . The Lineage
Does not provide a Holy Man to die—
By violence."

IV

He has gone down like a doomed
Bride to the low tower of his fate

unknown;
And like the sea sound at the bottom of a stair
Yellow with the phosphor that sleeks the stone
The road roars above the frescoed chamber of
His shattered head

(the world that *can* appear—
In which these words are read, the faint traces
Of disabled care).

The guide is dead

who used
To make his way through Waltham, as in a dream:
And now I sometimes do the same.

—Veda reader

Zil'berman, drowned Argonaut
Of our humid August of the awe and dust,
And ghost

it was a graceless sort of teaching
To get thus lost,

unless you have become
The truth you taught, the unapparent end
Of seeking—

(We did not kill you; nor the boy in the car.)

born to disappear.

V

O charioteer,
Release me from the burden of this speaking.
I am overcome once more by sleep, mere
Singer in a low chair with the one key

—"Hear me, Allen. Death is nothing you must fear."

That only scars the door.

Release me, David.
"Hear me, Allen. Death is nothing you must fear."

Release me

"Death is"

from the burden of the

"Nothing you must"

speaking—
"fear . . .

This is
The Prothanatïon of a Charioteer."

TO S—

Whenever I faintly imagined the face
Of my truest love (at last!)

suspended
In this the middle distance of my
Mind's dark, an

oval, reddish, glowing, hope
Diamond—
My own face, I think, when young

but bodiless,
Alight, a planet (not a star)
A serene, a near mark, a steady sight—

I said, "This is the long-awaited beginning
Of my love,"

and saw by the imagined light
Of the planet the mirrors of your eyes
With pictures in them of my own face young.

"I am loved," I said to you. "Loved," you said,
"By the light of the planet."

—Whenever I imagined
The bright face of my truest love at last,
The light increased.

It was a marriage gem,
My own face young which shone

in the dark.
"I am loved," I said. "Loved," you said to me,
"By this light."

—Whenever in mind the planet
Rises, love sweeps me into space

("Loved" "Loved")
Never to be quiet, as the poet said,
And not to die

(This is the beginning, long awaited.)—
And not to die, before my time.

THE SLAVE

And the angel of the Lord was by the threshing-
place of Araunah the Jebusite. II Sam. 24:16

I
Why must the poet rage?

Because of nations,
And the angels.—With my right hand I turn,
And turn the pages; and with my left hand note
This place.

Read, angels, if you can; and say
To the nations (Jerusalem, first of all)
The poet has sent a *s*ign,

a light blue
Romanza, the eloquence of water,
The sound of a girl talking with her friends.

I have come a long way to work out this:

II

—My left hand and right hand are not the same.

By contrast to my right hand, my left hand
Is clearly older, more worn.

My right hand
Seems innocent beside that other one—
Less, or differently, used; certainly,
More vulnerable.

(By the bad light of
Evening, at Jerusalem, in the blind heat
Of a June *sharav,* two glasses of pure
Water are infinitely differentiable.)

Witness the scythe-shaped scar—right index finger:
Witness the damaged nail of my right thumb.

This happened, as I now see, because my
Right hand held what my left hand worked upon,
And received the wounds.

Witness, also, the scar
In the pad at the base of my right thumb.

III
Nonetheless, my left hand is closer to death.
You can see in this half-
Light—the lines in the left palm make a mortal
M, a *morte.*

(Outside, under the flail-stone
And hot swingle of the iniquitous farmer,
Jerusalem, on the high threshing rock
The meticulous south wind sifts and sorts.
"Only this is," it says. "And this other
Is not anything.")

My right hand, despite the
Scars, is really asleep (but I do not
Know how to wake it);

and deep in my brain
Left and right hand are like two glasses of
Very pure water on a day when two
Glasses are enough.

The lines in the palm
Of my right hand form an X—no letter.

IV
Perhaps, that is why my left hand does this
Writing, or why when reading I lay my
Left hand on the page, and with my right hand
I support my head.

Outside, in the wild
Night, anyone who looks can see the floating
Islands of cloud darken the Via Dolorosa
And moonlit Gesthemane,

and carry a cool
Moment over the Mount to Bethany—
But at this season no rain.

The wind blows
Down my lamp; and it explodes on the floor.

This is the breaking up of the *sharav.*

V

Now, behold! A struck moon among the high
Grecian islands of shade—conscious scripture
Without letter;

and hear! The sinister farmer
At work in the lower dark—battering, battering:
"This is, and that other is not anything."

(Outside, the west wind is like a very beautiful
Girl, her two breasts

glasses of pure water,
The right slightly fuller than the left, as
She raises her left hand to adjust her hair.)

The sun rises behind the Dormition—where
Mary fell asleep—like lilies in full hands.

What is the beautiful girl doing now?

She is
Talking to her friends, a very beautiful girl
Who today will wear blue for the hot weather.

VI

Every nation has an angel. Most are pale;
And stand in their killing clothes night and day.

The angel of Jerusalem is pale,

and stands
At the highest pinnacle of the threshing
Rock teaching curses to the sinister farmer,
Jerusalem,

as the sun rises. The wind shifts to
The south, and begins to sort the night's threshing,
"This to life, and this other to the fire."

I do not study with the aim of saying
Trivial things.—If the angel of Jerusalem
Had human eyes . . .

If Jerusalem were a pool
Where a very beautiful girl might walk or sit,
As she pleased, or bathe . . . If the angel of
Jerusalem had ears for the light blue eloquence
of water . . .

But Jerusalem is a slave.
My left hand signs—"Death"; the right makes its mark.

THOSE PEARLS HIS EYES

Or, Pathologies of a Letter Unsent

PAUL WEST

Reread, it sounds loathsome; I just can't send his daughter something that begins, as this does, "When twin eyeballs arrived by registered mail, each resting on absorbent cotton in a pillbox, I transferred them by means of the cotton to a milkglass plate." And continues, "Then, alarmed by the reflection, I slid a sharp-edged sheet of typing paper, best bond, beneath; I do much the same with the finger-long house centipedes I spray to death in the basement, after which I tip the corpses outside on the patio. Next day they have gone, so perhaps over the years I have been infecting a tribe of chipmunks, or a chorus of cardinals, with DDT. Never mind. All of a sudden the watermark showed through like a filament, and I realized in full what I inertly knew: the eyes—those blue eyes of Manfred Vibber—were mucous, recent. And I slid the plate into the refrigerator next to the diet margarine. Incongruous, but I needed to think. In the event, I thought for several weeks.

"I am a mild man, unaccustomed to receiving eyes by mail, even from (or of) long-standing friends, and still less the eyes of other species. Notice how I refine a hypothetical distinction: mark, I'm told, of the timid. Be that as it may, I'm shortsighted too, mark (among other marks) of the Rare Book Curator, which of course I happen to be, have been these twenty years. I have written thousands of sentences, but I have collected and tended millions more, almost as if books were butterflies or birds' eggs. Except that they aren't, any more than they are eyes, although. . . . Picture, if you will, then, the astonishment when a rare book expert receives the eyes of that eminent physicist who devoted his prime to the field-ion and atom-probe microscopes, who, stranded after World War Two in the Russian sector of East Germany with a wife and a young daughter to feed, survived by collecting broken marble gravestones and dissolving the marble in hydrochloric acid to make carbon dioxide, which he then piped into ammonia for a couple of hours. The resulting ammonium carbonate he dried out and packed into little bags labeled 'Dr. Vibber's Finest Baking Powder.' Bicycling round the countryside, he bartered baking powder with the farmers for flour. Bread from headstones, as he said. He got the acid from the local pharmacy, easily because it wasn't edible, and the bucketfuls of ammonia at the city gas plant. How about that, I thought, for existentialism! But none of that is news to you. Or so I suppose. 'It is good to know a little chemistry,' he said, 'even if you are a physicist.' It sounded as if he were saying it is good to have moons if you possess a planet, and I, mainly for lack of something comparably definitive to add, just told him that if the library is the heart of a university, the rare book room is the heart of the library. Where I heard that first I no longer know; I say it here only to keep from repeating the obscene thought that came as I stared at the eyes: How do *these* rate in value against the Gutenberg Bible and, oh, to be vulgar, a First Folio of Shakespeare? Worse, how to classify them? As incunabula—artifacts of an early period? As novelty bindings, along with thumb-sized dictionaries and books with vignettes painted across the gold leaf of the page edges clamped together? With Lord's-Prayer-inscribed whaleteeth, bits of wall graffitied by Lord Byron, or, hideous to contemplate, Jivaro proverbs on shrunken foreheads? No, I resolved, if anywhere these belong among those snowglobes of the Statue of Liberty or the Golden Gate Bridge, and not in a rare book collection at all. Shake them—the globes—and a little blizzard begins in the enclosed water: a pretty enough bauble. Shake these—the eyes—and who knows what mind-boggling kaleidoscope of images will start? *Kak*eidoscope! Something hideous beyond belief. No, the images were really in your father's brain, weren't they, and where is that now? Not to mention his great mind. Pardon the liberty, I beg you; how else can I say anything at all, so long after the event?

"What began his trouble, if trouble is the word, was the short leave he took during the summer: a leave from research, not from teaching, for he rarely did anything so prosaic, and this we had in common. Since his account of the events was—how shall I put it?—dispersed, laconic, and plainly inconsistent, it's hard to be certain. Such eyewitnesses (I flinch at the very word) as there were seem to have vanished or lost interest, if indeed anyone really noticed him at all. There was no doctor on board, the one appointed having been felled by a coronary only hours before sailing, which was bad luck for him, worse for your father. On board what, you may have forgotten, and with reason (my fumbling recap threatens to become bungling). It was July, and your father had bought passage on the 23,000-ton Indonesian liner *Cusca Dam* in order to witness a total eclipse of the sun from the North Atlantic. The crassness of this so-called "Eclipse Special" amused rather than provoked him, and he was among the first to reserve one of the eight hundred berths costing, I think, one hundred and fifty dollars for the round trip.

" 'But,' I remember asking him, 'how good a view will you have? Out at sea?' The best view, I had read, would be from the north shore of the St. Lawrence River, about three hundred miles east of Quebec, at Godbout, Baie-Trinité, Ilets-Caribou, and in the Gaspé Peninsula between Matane and Mont-Louis. I told him this, jokingly: 'My middle name is information! I'm a mine of it. I don't just buy a newspaper, I read it front to back. Which means other people don't have to. I'm a relay station for data. My essence is to be of use.' He told me, not without some of that sardonicism without which campus life would be funereal, that it wouldn't matter. He'd see enough. He had to go, since this would be the last total solar blackout within easy access of the East Coast for forty-five years, although there would be a feebler one in 1979. I let the matter drop, only incidentally marveling at his passion for—perish the phrase—eyeball witness, bizarre when you consider the panoply of instrumentation at his command, not to mention the vast resources of information retrieval. Firsthand, that's what he wanted; and now, looking back, I can see why. Each time I brush my teeth before retiring for the night, I study my physique in the mirror, touch or palp it here and there, assuring myself that all the possibilities of death are here and now within this mass. Of all known mortal options, several are latent within this bolus of bone and blubber, water and muscle (a little), which I so familiarly call Me, just awaiting in the dugout the call to action. Once thought, such a thought becomes a repetend: obligatory daily, a hundred times over, even before nightfall. So I keep busy, buying two- and three-hundred-year-old books with university funds, spending the budget like water while my own tiny cells spend me.

"Using no mind at all, as Vibber—your father—himself said, he glanced away from his rectangle of smoked glass, forgot all he knew about imperative reflectedness, and looked right into the blanked-out sun, which at once seemed to recognize him. What it was that thus distracted him, not only from his learning in such matters but also from common sense, I never learned: maybe a flying fish dazed him into some amphibian delight, or a lurch of the vessel shifted his Indonesian-American cheeseburger sideways inside him, or (which I favor) an antique hubris surged up in him and Manfred Vibber, newborn as some kind of novel trinity, became Phaethon son of Helios attempting to drive the sun chariot, Icarus initiating his own sunflare air force, and Copernicus identifying the solar middle of things. The hub of the planetary cartwheel held him and transfigured him. About which I have only this to say: a wolf in sheep's clothing is still a wolf, which is why, I suppose, a man willing to offend his own sight can inadvertently become a solar cell, anthropomorphic variety; a sheep in wolf's clothing is still a sheep, which is why none of the other passengers—oblique heli-observers all—suffered the least ill-effect. How dismal I am making it sound, whereas really it was rather glorious.

"In fact Vibber struck gold; gold struck him. And thenceforth, even while denouncing his own recklessness, he spoke as one who had parleyed with mc^2 direct and no longer needed such indirect etiquettes of cosmic polish as the C. G. Gauss medal, the H. N. Potts gold medal of the Franklin Institute, the Medard W. Welch Award of the American Vacuum Society, not even half a Nobel Prize or enough chemistry to turn headstones into baking powder. Here is how I express it:

"Net Loss: In the first instance, sight for three days.

"Net Gain: An insight into the heart of things, which I know sounds sentimental, but optimistic cosmic conjecture usually is (see my earlier profundities about the heart of a university's being the rare book room, etc.).

"Synthesis: Everything that follows, even if, out of my incapacity to respond prudently to this retelling of a tale I have already appalled my so-called superiors with, I spin off into levity. I am such a man who, while asserting that men who repeat history aren't obliged to know any, repeatedly tries to open the door to his library vault with his Phi Beta Kappa key. Exclaims, 'Wrong key!' and so draws polemic attention to it.

"Enough of schematization. The denuded facts are that Vibber, in fact, did not receive medical attention until the ship returned to its West Side pier a day and a half later. For all that time he was blind, with a high fever. For three days and three nights, according to him, he neither saw, slept, nor ate, but remained in a hyperconscious trance, both aboard ship and in hospital, while his visual memory staged a riot and he felt as if his eyelashes were in-turned and piercing his eyeballs at baleful speed. Then, quite without warning, the needling stopped and his sight came back (while he was on the phone to his wife, your mother I mean); but all he said to her was, 'There now, I've switched back on again. Strangely enough. . . .' She, Hannah, took the last two words as the last in the sentence and sensed no points of suspension, as these things get fancily called. Relief precluded misgiving while she taxied at once from her hotel to the hospital. Soon after, she brought him home to Pittsburgh, where he prepared to spend his usual calm summer and—apart from some unprecedented outbursts of temper alternating with fits of invulnerable abstractedness—impressed her as none the worse for his mishap. Back to normal, he read the oculist's chart without error, kept his body at an exemplary 98.6 F., and experienced no headaches at all. Vibber, you might say, had come through once again.

"Or so he let people believe. One evening, over a bottle of sweet sherry in his booklined basement-laboratory (this mercifully free of centipedes), he told me a truth I could not, later, bear to recall while looking at the eyes. Ordinary vision he still had, of course, but supplemented. 'Not only,' he told me, 'am I seeing by polarized light, with all random vibrations eliminated. I'm also seeing everything in stupendous magnification. It's. . . .' His explanation made me shiver: Most people with normal vision can, with a little effort, blur their sight sufficiently not to be able to decipher print that is in front of them. The eye muscles relax, fail to focus. Now, to see normally at all, Vibber had to make this same focus-blurring effort, the results of which he laughingly compared to the 'habitation-fog' of Siberia. Otherwise he saw everything vastly and perfectly, and in electromagnetic context. He even made some joke about Rent-A-Scope, but I was too preoccupied for that with how his eyes and head must feel. But no, he said: no discomfort, not even a buzz. It was like some addable harmony added. What he saw he saw with mind's eyes. Neither ECGs nor EKGs revealed anything unusual, nor did the thorough medical which the university obliged him to submit to at fifty-five, as a member of what was unamusingly called 'the presenile generation.' Only once did I doubt him, dare to think him a liar (as if living up to the sound of his name, with F replacing V), and I at once reconsidered: he was gaining nothing beyond private satisfaction; no publicity; no new discoveries; no din from space to boast about. Why the sun had brought about what it had, to him a Lutheran believer, he had no idea; but it had, as he explained, enabled him to dispense with certain instruments. He was a walking microscope that rectified its own visible light and magnified unprecedentedly. 'At will,' he said, 'once I've switched over, I can see almost anything in detail. Right now, for example, a speck of oyster shell is burning into lime which, in a drop of seawater, precipitates magnesium hydrate! Sorry to be so technical. The main difference though, is that the speck is as big as Greenland and the drop is the size of the Pacific. I won't bore you with the process, but the end-product is magnesium. I can see it forming now.'

" '*Cui bono?*' I learnedly asked. 'What *good* is all this?'

" 'Confirmation only. Nothing I didn't know before.'

" 'Except,' I told him, 'you're doing it direct. It's as if—'

" 'Spare me the analogy.' His face was flushed with a boyish guiltiness. 'I am just receiving a more private version of the universe. Along certain lines only. I'm far from being complete.'

"Then, perhaps piqued with being interrupted, I asked him to envision and see plain and magnify God. I think he tried to, but he couldn't: not unless, he suggested with a flicker of malice, I regarded the divinity as elegantly interiorized low-range radiant energy. So I suggested he wouldn't receive this particular subject until he himself transmitted it: to be is to be perceived, I said, but he cut me off short, again, this time with some tag from Niels Bohr—Your theory is crazy, but not crazy enough to be true. The sherry was gone. Hannah was due to arrive home (and I have always avoided her for reasons—no, I will spare you those). To sweeten parting, however, he staged an event for me, in the course of which I saw, or thought I saw, or dreamed I thought I saw, or *pretended* I dreamed I thought I saw (as if the ammonite were to enlarge its spiral into the rooster tail of the Milky Way) the town of Trenton, New Jersey, coming to a halt as it neared the New York-Pittsburgh train; my own hand inscribing in long-hand the title page of a book apparently called *Journal of the Plague Year, A.D. 1;* a mile-long spermatozoon writhing up out of Death Valley with 'EDEN' lettered in black on its flank; and what I somehow knew was the Chinese character for 'peace' being let down from the sky upon the whole of Pennsylvania, smothering it quite, except for inlets and interstices through which smoke rose until even that stopped. I tell you; it looked like revenge.

"These things having been accomplished (as Julius Caesar used to say when introducing a new phase in his account of some campaign or other), he let me stew for a while, vouchsafing no information even when, for coffee or sherry, we were alone together. He seemed to have withdrawn into extraordinariness, and I, who have never developed smooth habits of talking (although I speak in an informative staccato mainly because almost everything I say I have said before, such is the nature of my calling), had neither the heart nor the skill to sound him. The summer waxed and bulged, its pollens found me wherever I went and (as usual) made both nose and eyes seep that awful seasonal histamine, mucus, lymph, whatever it is. Only in the blue-carpeted, air-conditioned fastness of the rare book room—Caxton's Morgue, as some of its facetious and ungrateful users dub it—could I find a relief that was also social, marshaling my small platoon of quietly spoken deft females, after none of whom I hankered, as if my divorce years ago had left me numb in that appetitive region of the brain. Three or four encounters, more or less furtive, over five years, and that has been it. I am in some kind of abeyance. Understand me, Miss Vibber, were the right occasion to present itself, under the best venereal auspices, I might not dawdle; but, thus far, the overtures of certain equally divorced Mistresses of Library Science, some with a brood of offspring, have not worked the trick or met my formula. Sugar I several times tasted, like a housefly at a table bowl, and no good it did me. The body needs it not. And now my tastes are sourer, and weirder, as is evident. It helps to write these things aloud.

"How sweet-sour, then, was the day he reeled into my bookish domain, breathless, haggard, and intermittently shading his eyes, these already protected by dark sunglasses. We withdrew into my sanctum, and I ordered some tea for him, although he seemed beyond all the power of tannic acid to restore. Still, you have to do something civilly accommodating on these occasions, even if it amount only to a china cup and saucer your guest ignores. With the cassette tape-recorder from my desk before us, and switched on at his request (it like some tabloid recording angel), he began to disburden himself with ceremony or, I might say, his usual diffidence writ large. You, his daughter, were away in Europe (the University of Montpellier, was it not? Your year abroad from the Romance languages as they are done at Cornell?), and I know he was never one to confide in Hannah, whose mind, pardon the frankness, has a sedentary stance I find gruesome. My asperities, I regret to say, are those of patience shredded. Forgive me too that I refer to your late father by surname, as if he were a distant institution: he *was*, even to his friends, especially to those who couldn't bring themselves to call him Manfred. And now he has become a monument. Back to my matter, which isn't that easy to control, not least because it is for your own eventual consumption. Indulge me, please.

"It seems that, over the period end-June through mid-July, his power of magnification increased and increased. He provided me with instances (I who still marveled at the event he had somehow staged in my own mind's eye), and I think that in his position I would have gone insane. Wandering into the kitchen late at night, after Hannah had gone to bed he opened the refrigerator door and momentarily, because he was hungry, allowed his willed, normal vision to slip. The skin of a part-sliced onion burst upon him like red-hot molten iron, spotted with silver lieutenant's-bars and patches of sapphire blue. But he persisted in trying to fix a snack, refused to acknowledge the silver Cuba-shaped island in the red-cabbage purple that was the faint mold on the bread. A flake of baked potato on the rim of a plate became an acre of buff flat pebbles scattered with cherry blossom, but he spurned it, only to be dazzled by the ocher-on-black galaxy of the mustard. So as not to be engulfed by the scales of an imported Portuguese sardine, he concentrated on one scale only, but found himself staring aerially down into a steep amphitheater in which all the seats were balconies. Sugar was a cumulus ball flooded with pastel rainbows. The milk he at last settled for poured into an egg-shape that became a fringed crater with a dozen tiny moons ascending from it in a perfect ring. So he decided to drink water, but it fell from the faucet as blue-glass paperweights, triangular, hexagonal, square, and the vitamin B-12 tablet he decided his nerves required came on strong as a loose assembly of scarlet feathers and small brown spatulas. And, as was rapidly becoming clear, while everything seethed and opened up, settled and then seethed again, gaudiness was becoming almost architectural. Second to second, he lived in a visual world that had too much in it. Every slightest thing was an act of God, outclassing earthquakes and thunderclaps, and he, who of all men should have been accustomed to visions, felt 'sore afraid' (his own words, but a long way from his usual idiom).

"There were worse reasons too. The staples he tried to fit into his stapler were a vermilion ribcage. Outsqueezed toothpaste was a violet quicksand above which he floated weightlessly. Being nylon, his pajamas revealed themselves as an endlessly interlocking grid of repeated capital omegas. The flame from the Bunsen burner in his basement wriggled with two waists and three pelvises. Brass of the ashtray frothed with all colors save red. A coin's nickel was a cliff quarried deep for corpses methodically stacked. The black plastic of his pen flaked, the flake was a squadron of eastward-plunging open-beaked sienna gulls. Out of an oak splinter soared basketwork torsos with maroon breasts. Facing Hannah over the counter between kitchen and living room, he saw himself upside down on her retinas, against a network of blood vessels and one bright spot that was the optic nerve.

"Mentally he enlarged himself to stay in proportion with what he saw. His other senses began to numb out. An ability to see by X-rays came to him, and he even began to project three-dimensional laser patterns.

"Completely polarized light became only one among his awful

privileges, like a stampeding of white bulls groomed into military single file, but then seen only as processing skeletons. He tried to be glad he was privy to the texture of the universe, glad about his growing powers, glad to be seeing with eyes almost divine. For a time he reveled in the purple cone-shells of DDT on the leaves in his terraced rear garden, hoping to steady himself by fixing on them and them alone, but everything else in his visual field trespassed on this devotion, scattering even the purple. And soon he felt even the unuttered language resist him, which is to say he no longer thought words (not without enormous effort) but looked volumes. Yet one word, esoteric and therefore rarely abused, he held to, as his talisman: *aliunde,* meaning 'from a source extrinsic to the matter at hand.' By this word he intended (I think) both the grotesque build-up of his eyes' power and the invasion of his view by things not even being looked at, but also Mother Nature's supplanting of his laboratory hardware. I am tempted to say that all this made him see red—there, I've said it. Of course he was angry, but he was also awed at having been singled out with only minor lobbying on his part. Of *aliunde,* really a legal term, he spoke freely, and I later came to realize it meant possession by a god: what used to be called enthusiasm. Rational as he was, he seemed also, although resentfully, to be succumbing to fervor, somewhat along these lines: Divine Design was martyring him, yet to no purpose other than the restoration of humility (something I estimate he never lost, remembering as I do the baking soda and the headstones).

"Panopsis invaded his dreams as well. Sometimes he saw, although larger and more clearly, things he had already seen through his microscopes; but sometimes things homed in on him from the boundaries of human knowledge, attracted to him by vibration or even chance. The amino acid named glycine, for example, he already knew as resembling interlocked prisms and lozenge-shapes fringed by salmon-hued fernwork. But how, without having seen them before, did he recognize the frogspawn-textured maroon lamb chop as a section of umbilical cord, or that stunning white antlered stag, upside down against purple and royal blue, as a sliver of the human bladder? The colors, as any microscopist knows, were arbitrary, but not the shapes. Similarly, he saw a blood clot, hand-sized (or as large as Latin America, he wasn't sure), inside a fat-constricted aorta; a cross-section of Amiens Cathedral, being subjected to the pressures of a gale, reproducing in its iridescence parts of the human anatomy, here a naveled belly, there two muscular legs; and, most astounding of all, a leaf-thick tree scarlet from the infrared its leaves reflected, with the sun itself shining through the branches like a Christmas card star. No one principle obtained: night and day, he saw in slow motion and through time-lapse, telescopically and its reverse, by means of ions and neutrons and holographic lasers. Too much. Never, I gathered, were your father's retinas vacant. The more he told, the farther my own mind traveled in search of some counter, some principle, that would make sense of him. I thought of fishermen taking carp by archery, or with pitchforks, near the picnic tables of flooded parks. I recalled Goethe's little book about colors. I vaguely considered Glanvill's argument for Adam's having had both telescopic and microscopic vision, but dropped it as fatuous. I prefer the man who said that we see the Milky Way because it exists in our souls, not so much a flashback as a flashforward. You can see how exercised I was.

"Then I drew back, fearful of Vibber's perceptual abysses. Let him leap into the blistering bowels of his own Etna; I would meanwhile scout the rim, diligently rehearsing the current prices of certain rare books. I apologize for the seeming incivility of thus referring to your father, but it is a pain to set these matters down; I have only one view of the matter, and only one epistolary style. Not long after he left me on that confessional day in high summer (he unconsoled, I dismayed), he was discovered in the nuclear reactor building peering down into the 71,000-gallon pool, murmuring something rhythmical at the blue glow of the Cerenkov radiation. Persuaded to leave, he vowed to return when he felt better, but to the cobalt-60 facility next door, 'as a human sample. After all,' he said, 'the gamma rays can sterilize or cause mutations, but they don't make the sample radioactive!' I am amazed he had enough words left to say anything of the kind. Urged home finally, as you must know, he never emerged again. It was as if, at fifty-five, he died of old age, at accelerated speed, over three or four days. The pneumonia I regard as a symptom, not a cause, but what I am less certain about is the absence of anything unusual in the medical reports until, in accordance with his will (the bizarre nature of which you will appreciate), the eye hospital forwarded his 'unacceptable' eyes to me. A last thrust? A cannon-shot in dirty pool?

I will never know. In the final analysis, I am grateful he remembered me at all.

"As Curator, that is. Which brings me to the arrangements I have now made. This is not the Museum of Natural History or the Rostand Institute of Biological Sciences: we are book people, and our facilities are for rare books. We dote on print. Emboldened, however, by libraries around the world that have, say, curls of the poet Shelley's hair, a piece of Arthur Rimbaud's kneecap, one of Rasputin's hands (not to mention, at one extreme, fragments of the Holy Grail, and, at the other, unmentionable anatomical relics of Napoleon), I have at long last had the eyes enclosed in perspex spheres, mounted on black velvet atop a marble plinth, and the entire artifact in a transparent refrigerator the size of a shoebox. We curators have to move with the times. This is centrally displayed in the rare book room on campus and will soon be backed by a bust now in commission. I trust you will find these dispositions suitable. We now have more visitors than ever. Sincerely yours, Virgil I. Proneskewer/Chief of Special Collections."

Such lies I tell. Of course I cannot send it to her: it begins with, and persists intermittently in, callous impersonality as if she weren't there at all; it addresses her directly much too late; it harps on things she already knows (and which no doubt explain her renewed absence abroad); it is miserably *couched;* and I seem continually to be getting in my own way. All of this is Vibber's fault no doubt. Use it, then, for something else, such as a resignation. It is the perfect flesh out of which to carve such a thing. To hell with protocol: you do not explain resignations. When you have to go, you just go. Submit it as it is. These words, I, and Vibber's eyes, must go together, we have none of us been taken seriously, especially by the campus bureaucrats. They said their nay, but oh the eyes have it. All I hope now is that my new collection, in Boston, will have room. A new post at my age is no mere bagatelle. I pray that the faculty there doesn't sport an eclipse-visiting eunuch, otherwise. . . . But the next total eclipse beyond the end of this document isn't until 2017, by which time I am certain to be in other hands, under different auspices, and no longer, by one of the deity's proxies, eyed.

TWO POEMS

GUSTAF SOBIN

BREATHHERD

1

. . . . blown snows
lacing the
high precipices, Robion
ocherous, beneath, I
blew the

lamb-
transparent, in
loose

ripples, before me. . . .

•

flared
ground, fanned
thrush, in shadows the
treasured
ice.

were tethered
inseparable, wed for-
ever to these
bone-

less
drafts, the driven
interval's.
breath-

herded up-
wards, onto the
worn, wind-
riddled ledges, your

bells
beat silent

off my vaporous horn.

2
nothing that
was, wasn't twice. . . .

wandered,
charred

white, over the
spine-

eyed thistles, to
tell you, my tousled
angel, *holly,*
ivy,
acorn,

words
that you'd never hear.

•

a last
village spread, in a
fresco of
glazed angles, before
us. . . .

geese
jeered at the
moon's

wizened crib.

you were, and
weren't.
were the heavy tuft of
my darkness, come
un-
done. . . .

cracked
walls, coarse sheets!
in

that tall
glacial room, to
lay my-
self down, the length of
those

cold oils, quick
fleece, the
breath

reach rooted

into
the radiance it breathes.

AND THUS UNTO

"... that the earth might be made
sensible of her inhuman taste . . ."
—Djuna Barnes

"ne la perds pas"

1
flares chestnut, in
deep gusts
of wind. . . . is *their* world, Saint
Sulpice, the
whispers,

clicking dice-
like, mix

with our voices, rotate
through
the milky
astringent jade. . . .

•

that even the
bones, our

least breath, be
swept

into those speculated wastes. . . .
(way that, spread-
winged, the

puffed marble, the
stars
at the tip
of their stiff petals flutter,
hesitate).

•

as if. . . .
as if, in
that breaking, the
vocable

would open,
ave-
vacuous of the eternally deferred.

in jars the
creams, thin disks the
rouge, rubbed in
taut ovals
over the flush of your cheeks.

2
Paris
arboreal, its
bough
of dense mirrors
blown into branches, invisible
beaks.

are as
if gathered,

lifted. . . . the
limbs

as they
grapple: point.

what pigments, the
flaked bells
of whose robes would float—whipped
gold—across
all that
abandoned decor?

•

Sèvres-
Babylone; in
updrafts,
off

your
tall forehead, your
soft horns

scroll. to
speak
of that stillness; to see you, and

still speak.

•

worlds un-
ravel
worlds, the
wrought heavens. . . . our blanched
reflectives.
would

leave, who'd
perched, already, a tribe-in-
flight, at the
breath's

flaked
edges.

•

weight-
less that
gaze, a

gray fume, chaliced
in ivory. . . .

that the brush
catch
on its fires; the night climb,
light, a light-
articulate, off our tapered fates.

MY MOTHER WALKED OUT

MICHAEL HANNON

My mother walked out.
My mother pointed her shoe.
I clung to my mother.
Crude logic conned the knife.
I fell.
Filthy life swam up and kissed the sun.
I looked down at my feet.
The abyss was humming with milk and Jesus.
My mother pointed her shoe at the roof.
The roof caught on fire.
I filled the cup of my birth.
I looked down at my feet.
Smashed rock pulled down the sky and seared it.
I mouthed a sentence.
Behind me the axe bit into the crucifix.
I was out but still holding on.
I switchbacked up the ridge looking for a hog.
I found it before it found me.
I ate it.
It was good bristly meat.
I looked down at my feet.
The sea went under a glacier.
The stars came out fighting for pieces.
The stars turned inside out.

The stars filled my cells with water.
I couldn't go anywhere without the stars.
I heard singing in the house.
I heard someone crashing in the brush.
I felt the sun coming a long way off.
I followed the furrow my mother left.
The light ate the flowers.
I wanted to be good.
I wanted to make something.
The propeller lifted my mother's skirt.
I saw her meat.
It made me crazy.
They crossed my legs.
I had to crouch in the library.
I looked down at my feet.
The rattlesnakes ate the light.
I held the dead jockey in my arms.
I read Rimbaud.
I wanted to win.
I looked down at my feet.
The teacher was kissing a penis.
My mother pointed her shoe.
The school burned down.
I was frightened.
I wanted to swallow my mother's feet.
My mother said it didn't matter.
I woke up in the dark.
I went to my mother's room.
My mother wasn't alone.
I asked God not to take my mother.
God gave me an earache.
I screamed and screamed.
My mother held me.
My mother told me.
God didn't have any meat of his own.
I screamed.
The pain was unbearable.
The bone man came.
The bone man cut out the bad part.

It hurt my mother.
I looked down at my feet.
My mother spun the ego.
A coin hit the whiskey glass.
My mother baked the bread.
It came out funny.
I ate it.
It made me crazy.
My mother split the atom.
My mother danced in the air.
The people all turned black.
She said it didn't matter.
I wasn't sure.
I wasn't sure of anything.
I looked down at my feet.
The crowd swayed the boardwalk.
My mother was in a hurry.
I held my mother's hand.
She found the right man.
She took him into the mirror.
I looked down at my feet.
The boardwalk made holes in the ocean.
My mother came out of the mirror.
She was twice as beautiful.
She was alone.
I helped my mother put on her shoe.
I looked up her dress.
There was blood on her teeth.
The police were looking for my mother.
They didn't know where to look.
My mother was asleep on the ocean.
I looked down at my feet.
I pretended to be dead.
Somebody said the penis was God.
My mother got dark in the face.
My mother spoiled the harvest.
My mother got into the animals.
My mother made them swell up.
My mother turned over the horse.

My mother hid me in the ruined corn.
She plowed the starry field.
She rubbed her bottom in the wheat.
Twisters surrounded the small town.
Minnows lept out of the preacher's bucket.
Catfish glowed in the dark.
My mother took one look at the river.
The river buried the storehouse.
The river carried off the pigs.
I looked down at my feet.
It was cold.
My mother ate all the blankets.
My mother got into the dog.
My mother made the dog sing all night.
My mother got into the television.
She made it talk sense.
My mother scattered the suitcase on the mountain.
The lingerie whispered to the moon.
My mother sent for the rat.
My mother sent for the rainbow snake.
My mother rubbed me with camphor.
My mother filled the kitchen with squash.
I looked down at my feet.
I couldn't believe what I saw.
I got drunk.
The moon went out.
The trees flew away.
I walked the black country road.
I found my father.
He was carrying a red ball of words.
He was old.
I took it from him.
I kissed my father.
My mother came down from the attic.
She was old.
She was very beautiful.
My mother kissed me.
I walked out.
I never looked back.
I looked down at my feet.

YAËL

From Volume IV of *The Book of Questions*

EDMOND JABÈS

Translated from the French by Rosmarie Waldrop

TRANSLATOR'S NOTE. *All of Edmond Jabès's books are about the word, about man defining himself through the word against all that threatens his existence: death, the infinite, silence, or our symbol for all these—God, our primal opponent.*

In Yaël *and* Elya *(volumes IV and V of* The Book of Questions*), the word takes the shape of a woman, Yaël. This woman cannot be faithful because the word implies the possibility of lies and ambiguity. The narrator, her lover, thinks he has killed her in his rage against the* other, *in his rage for truth. But one cannot kill the word. Only the child of their union, Elya, is stillborn, is silence. Truth is not for us, is not compatible with life. And the narrator, looking for his truth through the word, finds that he is being changed by the word, that he is turning into the* other. *He dies into his words, into his book. The creator dies into creation. Hence the book is also the death of God.*

Given this complex relation between man and the word it is not surprising that Jabès does not use traditional narrative. The naïve confidence in the thread, in the continuity of temporal and causal sequence, is lost. The story emerges out of a constant shift of voices, commentaries, and aphorisms. And the breaks between them "let the margins breathe," allow the white of the page, allow silence to speak. "In these breaks," said Maurice Blanchot, "the void becomes achievement . . . and thought shows through."

The Long Dialogue of Centuries

"All limits are dependent on light. Is God not the first, the original dark, in that case?
"And the first light to fathom the dark?"

"God is the all-embracing center."

The other is the savage sense of the sun.

"The light shows many a kindness to the lie, yet truth is in the light."

"The dark is dead passion, destroyed desire. Night love the night with its radiance in mourning."

"Silence is truth. Refusing to make allowances, it allows us to see.
"God is silence."

"God does not see. He is entrenched behind what is seen."

"God cannot be held back. He is the extreme of inconceivable sight."

"And extreme darkness which gives us to ourselves in absence."

"The invisible is both the renunciation of the lie and the will toward the only truth."

"Mute melody of worn memories. Rust is fire on vacation. From the beginning, the hour has trusted the sea."

"The hour in its darkness is a binary measure. We live in two times. Presence and absence take turns as its face."

"And neither face ever rules the other. So that the truth of the hour is a dizzying lack of being."

". . . an oblique opening."

"So that man in his flesh and his thoughts exists where eternity leaves him behind."

". . . where God is man's Truth which He withdraws."

". . . because death is life's first blood."

". . . because death is a second life of God."

"Thus the instant gradually became the breath of the creature that burns and consumes himself in his breath."

"Life continues beyond the day. Chased out of the garden in order to regain it (it will not be the same garden; it will only look the same) the instant, in every pulse beat of the world, is a rhythmic word.

"Thus the tree is aglow with a thousand similar words."

"Truth is often rhythm. Man and universe participate in one joint existence."

"The hour repudiates the hour, and eternity grows."

"The margins are the lip of the well of time where death draws water."

"Thus a river pushes at the weakest point of the bank. And the grass grows and bends with the same water, with long patience."

"So flows time outside time."

"Do we pay for the sin of knowledge by having our eyes torn out? Appearance condemns us to appearance."

"Impossible truth. Invincible truth. The possible carries truth, but outside its limits."

"Going toward truth means going all the way. It seems crossing all borders in order to look at them from the other side. Truth remains what is reached."

"Worthy conquest of man where God takes refuge, rejected from His Creation."

"God is not in the hand held out to another hand."

"Grasping means accepting things as they appear, imposing and exchanging them in their conventional form, appreciating the latter as the only form or pretending o . . ."

"Reality is not in our hands. Touching a thing, our fingers and palms play at creating the illusion of a reality which can be caught in its still movement."

"How ingenious desire is in its forms and caresses."

"Lies obey our touch. The senses have disqualified God and his essential insensibility, but have consecrated man without God."

"The body remains a crossroad."

" 'Cut off the hands,' howls the fool year after year. 'So that the eyes will kindle.' "

"What is not grasped has all the chances to become real."

"We chat, waiting for time. Alas, we are only marking time."

"Thus the word hardened as it lasted."

"Thus the stone became flint.
"Anything expressed is above all a rose of sound. And the world will never fit in a word."

"And God is never One and the same as you approach."

"Each for himself and both fused in the crystal of an idyllic mirror. Seen, but not delivered."

"Identity is distant. What is contemplated begins to contemplate."

"Any fruit is an artificial star. You taste the manure of the abyss. And soon the birds take off in fright."

"Where are we when we fall silent? The word is the presence of a forgotten presence."

". . . and the first gulp from the well and the course of the divide."

"But what is promised soon grows dim here, as if the infinite were a crowning feast."

"But here the mirrors band together to reflect endlessly man's last cry, his final cry for help. Here, the world in falling destroys the world."

"Here man brings suit against the word on which he has thrown himself for the most beautiful love song."

"Here man, with his soul in despair, leaves the word and shivers."

"Distance is the truth of speaking."

"The wall with its coat of plaster is eaten by the sky. Thus glaciers rise in the whiteness of death.
"O harsh bed of snow, calm rind amazed by transparency."

"Sheltered from the day, man confronts his shadow."

"We shall celebrate gardens. Spread mirrors. Glorify God."

"God is at the back of the mirror and at the heart of the tree."

"And the word, beseeched and denied, will be the ax man lifts against God."

"And man will perish by the ax."

"O time of the Witness, red spider silence."

The Three-Paneled Mirror

God wears a mask of nobility.

There cannot be any wounds caused by truth. Only the lie can touch us.
We are struck by our truth, but the truth rejects it.
So man turns to God and blasphemes. And the blasphemy falls back on him.
For God is the dawn of an exhausted wing.

A mask on a wall: maybe our face against eternity.

You will die in a mirror.

1

"He is the One who sees things as they are," man was told when he despaired of seeing.

In the first mirror, she smiles. She thinks of the treasure in her womb, of the life she is handing on and whose image moves her.

She has been in this village for six months. Waiting. Nobody has come to see her.

She looks out of the window at the hilly landscape where the trees are still asleep on their feet. The sun is barely coming up.

In the second mirror, her scream has cracked the glass—or was it the object she thought she had thrown at the door so that her landlady should hear?

People are fussing around her. A doctor and two peasant women.

"She has to be taken to the hospital. It's urgent," orders the doctor. Twenty or thirty miles away.

In the third mirror, the void engulfs the room.

Thighs spread wide.

The lips of the void, a vagina, huge.

Moist at the call of the phallus, bleeding as it rejects the world.

Life gambled and lost.

A dead infant, a box with a broken lock.

What was in this casket of scorn?

Roads and roads and roads.

A thousand beings die with every newborn.

There is rotten fruit among the seed.

2

A conspicuous milestone on the road to death.

The first.

You will go from face to face, but your breast will never feed the child of love.

Maimed mother.

The child you wanted to rock remains the most loved.

The creature atones.

In the first mirror, o woman, the lie relished its spite.

In the second mirror, o woman, the lie blew up.

In the third mirror, o woman, truth questions itself.

3

She has eyes of stone in the falling rain.
I do not yet exist.

Stretched out across the dark
she records, rolls into a ball.

What if space were only an immense yawning dawn?
God is bored.

4

In the first mirror, childhood found the garden laid waste.
In the second mirror, innocence found the roots in flame.
In the third mirror, it is dark, so dark that you tremble.

You will go from image to image, for God's amusement.

5

An insect tests the circle of light, a bird the basic line.

The dark speaks to the dark:

"Choosing means fixing? Then the lie is the night of choice."

"If reality lies in choice only the day is real."

"You grasp. You finger. You grope.
"You bring on day."

"Black oil, night of how many stories? Stain, stream, surah?

The dawn speaks to the dawn:

"Does every thought rest on a vegetable wager?"

"Time has the body for witness."

"Sea anemone, garden made of flowering water."

"You will die. Time will not see itself again."

Man speaks to man:

"Always the book and me. Unavoidable confrontation."

"The soul is a breath of death, a head airy with eternity."

You will go from word to word into the silence of God.

6

She noted:

"I looked out of my window at the mountains where the trees were studding the sky with stars."

She noted:

"Tree, I can see you.
You lie to my eyes.
I know you by the slant of your looks.
Not your existence: your impertinence."
"Who is more impertinent than a liar?"
"You lie to my mind.
Yet truth is *before* or *after* pact and seeing
or perhaps *between*.
Tree, I watch you.
Struck by your smallest trait.
Every day I feel closer to you
in what you are not and what your name designates.
Tree, I am growing with you,
with wanting to love
your bark and leaves."

7

The garden has folded its wings on us. Warm dark of the nest. The branch broke. Morning caught us helpless.

You will go from penny to penny until the end of time.

"And you will be blind. And you will rock the boat. And you will hate each other because of her and you will love each other to the bitter end. I shall be pleased not to see and to die of myself in your retinas."

Thus speaks the Voice in the time of absence.

The Garden

Seeing now means seeing only Nothing.

God's knowledge is in the tree.

Hence Nothing rules All. God is Nothing. Nothing is a ring.

I shall lead you into death and we shall forget the age of gardens.

1

Wisdom of symbols. A book which makes us see is a book of great wisdom.

You will make my body your favorite garden.

Every grain in its rich hours has to make the grade of a spiked lure.

Thinking about the terrestrial paradise leads us to a reflection on gardens.

Man and woman had for their prelandscape a park cultivated by the Lord.

Trees would have come into being before the animals if the latter had not been sure of a body even while still absent.

With an exemplary subtle touch, every inch of seeded ground perpetuates a human moment across the asides of form which are its symbolic avenues. As if the body were eternity.

Henceforth the couple will subdue the world with their intuitive return to the beginnings. They will see and carry on for the universe.

The lie is at its ease among plants. With its help, leaves and flowers resemble one another. The lie reproduces the same face.

Man is a reflection of the garden.

2

Truth is a leaven to God's hate. For a truthful being is His equal.

Paradise lost is followed by deserts where truth, the virtue of the sand, refutes the attributes of God.

Death opens the book with which man counters death.
God is against God.

3

We must give death time to learn how to die.

4

The daydreams of people walking in a garden wrap it in a silken melancholy which is ruffled by the cold as much as by the sun.

On cloudy days, hunched under their umbrellas, people look only at the ground.

Flowers, bright-colored cups. In spring and summer they owe their perfume to their liquor. In fall and winter, water and snow break them and hoot.

A child does not listen to trees. He makes them listen, draws them into his games.

Innocence of ambush. Revolt and resignation wear the same gala uniform. Parade without surprise.

The rainbow frays in the dumb reminiscences of shading.

Painting is a shared promise. A body is a nimble palette on legs (interchangeable brushes) to walk around the world. Until night is unsealed by sleep. O dream of dreams.

The daydreams of people walking in a garden turn into brown spittle on the branches, into dew on the leaves.

The blue of the sky is the blue of the space inside roots. It turns green in trunk and stem. The fruit swells with the infinite.

Up there, the dark makes sure of the harvest. Wheat is feverish like a flame. Gathered. Winnowed. The grain sparkles.

How winning the stars. They already smell the bread of dawn.

5

Parks have their fountains where thirst gives way.

Children have their favorite gardens. Likewise the walkers who come to inquire after the progress of vertigo in the soul of plants.

Is it the secrets the plants tell us which deliver them into our hands? Then everything would be words, and landscape the forms caught by the ear.

6

A gathering of young girls is the body of my beloved.
My mouth and fingers cull their words.

This morning, bench after bench full of girls.
A garden is the body's true world.

Girls whispering, singing, laughing.
The sad girl, is she a tear?

The more mysterious: the more voluptuous.
How small they are all to have room in one.

Yet it is the body wins out over life.
Not thought, nor pressing acts, nor work.

Radiant body, the blind man's kingdom.
What is the body? Do we ever ask?
It gives in to the eye from outside, to the hand in cahoots, gives in like the world.

Well-kept secret: the world was never more than a mooring-buoy in the night.

7

Saved by the unknown, man plunges into the unforeseeable. He has no recourse but ignorance with its boastful beacon. To see by the pinhole beam.

Beautiful summer of death.
O sun of endings.

8

That face of undefinable hunger which we must resemble, is that the soul?
Tragic duplicity of our features.
God flees.

Our eager hands try in vain to hold Him back and, coming together, outline the oval of His vanished face.

9

A lie: false start of truth?
An unhappy truth, then.
Or a good start but which, in the heat of action, in full career, loses interest in the goal or, rather gradually substitutes other goals until it is formally replaced.
But for whom?

Lie: trump of profit, space where truth explodes into myriads of counter-truths which man lights up with a short-lived life.
The creature is overwhelmed.

At the end of dreams truth kills itself. The lie triumphs.
Heyday of suicide.
You cannot count on anything.
You only survive ashes.

10

A thousand earthen octopuses devour the universe.
The tree's wound is the same as the ocean's.

Was my truth the anchor of my life?
I find myself where I fell asleep.
Yaël, waking bears your name. And your body is a long shiver of amorous flights.

11

The walker dissolves into his journeys. Years are towlines carried off by the current. The ground is suddenly no longer solid where the rose bends to look at itself. So little water. So much. Thirst performs the miracle of giving the world the privilege of dreams.
To drink. To drink the air, the dark, the day.

12

A life without miracles is doomed to the dullness of stagnant water. It has the dragonfly's capers to wake it.
On a different, but equally reduced plane, dust knows from birth the feel of downtrodden old age.
Rejected, it only irks our itinerary. Exile is its rest.

13

A garden stripped by the sun gives little jumps of modesty full of fragrance.

The leaf defends itself against the branch, and the flower against the stem's invitation to exhibit herself. Pranks of the birds, a piece of invisible clothing in their beaks.

The star you discover is perhaps a pale cry of love.

14

In the garden I do not have my tree. I have neither familiar bench nor flower,

no man or woman for company.
I have nothing.
Complex net of rest.
We do not get off the earth.
I wait for oblivion within me,
oblivion with clipped wings.

15

The man walking in the garden passed Yaël: God revealing Himself as a woman or Satan with the clear eyes of God.

The trees had brought her. The grass sighed under her feet.

Shadow of a twig? Shadows are dark daggers. This is why the murderer throws away his weapon once the crime is done.

Everywhere.

But what murder are we talking about?

Will I get the better of the unscrupulous mouth, pirate pupils, mutinous breasts and hands?

Truth is the order of the dying.

FIVE POEMS

LEONARDO SINISGALLI

Translated from the Italian by W. S. Di Piero

TRANSLATOR'S NOTE. *The poems in Leonardo Sinisgalli's early books (*18 poesie *appeared in 1936,* Vidi le Muse *in 1943) bore much of the characteristic "antieloquence" which had come to identify the literary movement known as Hermeticism. In critical discussions he was accordingly grouped with Montale, Ungaretti, Gatto, and Sereni, all of whom were for a time associated with the movement. Sinisgalli's work was distinguished by his preoccupation with memory and with rural custom and chthonic myth, the roots of which may be traced back to Greek antiquity. Montemurro, the town in Lucania where the poet was born and raised (and which is evoked in "Village"), figures in many of his poems as a place of mythic origins, with archaic traces or signs everywhere, a locale which one of his critics has called "a privileged space, remote, outside time." Sinisgalli published numerous collections of verse in his lifetime, as well as stories and essays. His major collections of poetry are* Poesie di ieri: 1931–1956 *and* L'ellisse: 1932–1972. *He was born in 1908 and died in 1981.—W. S. Di P.*

VILLAGE

We walked all around the village
while the donkeys were coming back loaded down with wood
from the sweetsmelling heights of the Serra,
scraping their hairy ears against the rough
walls of the houses. A bell tinkled on the neck
of a kid-goat, led by an old man
through the darkness like a dog. Someone
sitting in front of a door said goodnight.
The streets are so narrow and furniture
crowded so close to the doorways
that when the moon rose we could smell peppers
sizzling in pools of oil.

The color of the mountains excited you.
"Maybe they've been under water for thousands of years."
"Down here even the stones look withered,
even the leaves look a little tattered."
Women walked from houses with burning brands.
"In our village the sun sinks fast,
night begins when the noon bells ring."

Horses returning from the watering troughs
snorted, dogs prowled the doorways.
We were alone, treading the airborne ashes.
"It's as if everybody goes underground
to sleep then comes back to life
each morning." The street was quiet,
wrapped in rags, colorless.
In one locked house the tribe's billygoat
sneezed in Margherita's bed.

"Let's go visit the old folks. My aunt
and uncle always keep something good set aside
for me." We sit in the kitchen and see
the magical family of keys hanging on the wall:
the small garden key, the gigantic cellar key

over a hundred years old. "My grandfather
used to quiet all the screaming kids
by whistling through the keys." Here's the silvery key
to the rabbit hutch, and the oil lamps, lanterns, wicks.
I watch my family profiled,
magnified on the walls, and the enormous
shadows of flies creeping like mice.
"My grandmother, Cosima Diesbach, sailed around the world."
"*My* ancestors probably saw Atlantis."

At night Domenico comes to lock the churches
and bolt the gates of the dead.
"They used to tell us kids
that he talked to the owl, on the rooftops, up there.
The bellman is stone deaf
and sleeps hard. To lay out the dead
(he's better at it than anyone)
you had to call for hours
in the middle of the night and whistle loudly
through the keys." Domenico stands there,
strikes a match on his trousers, smokes his pipe,
engrossed on the edge of the deep ravine
where one night long ago I saw them set down
the casket of the dead Christ, by the railing.

Down in the valley Crescenzio goads his lame
mule. "I take things as they come."

WE'VE SPENT SO MANY NIGHTS

We've spent so many nights
In the loft above the threshing floor,
Our hands buried in wheat,
Sleeping while the dogs watched.
Your feet were gentler

Than the doves we made
From the white cloth of handkerchiefs.
There were wisps of straw in your hair;
You turned, and the field at your back
Quivered and rang.

PASSIONFLOWER

It's still ours, this fading
Evening light, a glare
On the crowns of the holm oaks. The fire
Burns in our room (a muffled
Rumbling snaps your vigil)
And as soon as it licks you
Your dress blazes: passion
Shields you from the flame like the leaf
Of an evergreen. You tremble
As the north wind
Ravages the orchards,
And behind the ashen window mourns
The torpid passionflower.

NIGHT OF SHOOTING STARS

I go back up to the hills
(they shimmer with wheat bent by the August breeze).
Silvestro, dear friend, you deliver me
To all things past, to the stress and toil
That wears the stone smooth over the grain,
And you offer me a leaf in your generous
Hand. You stand inside
The young moon's lazy halo,

Talking about all the right things.
The crisp wind flickers in your eyes
And harness bells jangle on the hilltops.
The enchanted crowds I saw ablaze
Are the lights of San Lorenzo. You laugh
When I fret over the long trail
Of ants you're burning.

CHESTNUT TREES

They laugh in my face
because I'm still thrilled
by chestnuts blossoming
in the July sun.
A breath of wind
shivers the clusters
like cats' tails.
Here and there in the dark green
of the oaks and the light green
of poplars and elms
the lush hairy
sulphur-yellow bundles
are blooming.

ACCOUNT

MELINDA CHATAIN

During the first course, a cold mousse of shellfish with watercress sauce, the man from Bolivia spoke of his torture and imprisonment. The only sound was a clinking of forks slicing down through the mousse, more a pâté than a mousse, dense and pale under the chilled green sauce, perfect for a hot June night. On the other side of the table, an estranged couple, not looking at each other, pushed the food to the sides of their plates. More wine was poured. "Of course you must understand that I was never physically tortured," said the man from Bolivia.

"And you were in jail how long?"

"Two months."

"Did they arrest you right after your return?"

"Oh, no! It was nearly a year. During that time I lectured at the university, always suspect, but I engaged in no political activity of any kind."

"So you thought you were safe."

"Well—"

"Excuse me, but I don't understand why you went back to Bolivia," said a young woman with a determined, professional, wide-eyed look; she opened her eyes yet wider as she asked her question.

"Yes, it's hard to explain. I spent the entire ten years of my exile putting out feelers, making connections to certain people in high places, to find out if it was plausible to return. My wife and children were horrified; they wished to stay where we were. But I began to receive assurances—not only assurances but there was talk of a government post!—and so we went back."

"You must have believed yourself to be fairly safe."

"Inasmuch as one can be safe in Bolivia."

"Still—" said the wide-eyed girl.

"They left you alone for almost a year?"

"Completely. Except that now and then they would approach me over the possibility of my taking a cabinet post, though they knew I had been a leftist."

"Then, out of the blue—"

"Yes. And my release was the same." He paused.

Directly across from the man from Bolivia, a florid-faced man, fanning himself, said, "It seems a pretty elaborate way to get turned down for a job."

The hostess gathered plates apologetically.

"Elaborate! Yes," said the man from Bolivia. "Those two months were the most elaborate of my life; so complicated, such an intricate design! They make the rest of my existence, past and future, seem airy and childlike. The elaborate things men do to each other—" He looked down as the main course was set on the table, poached chicken with a light mushroom sauce, set off by a garniture of seasonal vegetables cut very thin: leeks, carrots, asparagus. The host opened two more bottles of wine using a gunlike device that pumped air into the corks, exploding them out with little pops, sparing the ear the unpleasant rasp of cork against glass.

"The elaborate things men do," went on the man from Bolivia. "I was amazed to see how advanced my own country was in psychology, in this matter of psychological torture. I think perhaps it was my constant amazement that kept me sane those two months. But this is exceptional. You must have worked very hard," he said to the hostess.

"It's my hobby," she said, looking down.

"The very first day I was in prison," he said, "I had a three-hour interview with the prison director, an urbane and friendly fellow who spoke politely to me. Our interview was a model of civilized discourse except that we were circled constantly by *Chulumanos*, half-Indians from the Cordillera Highlands who, I must admit, have a reputation for bestiality. The director warned me that he had no control over the *Chulumanos,* that these were particular savages and sadists foisted off on him by the government to do as they liked with the prisoners. He himself would flinch each time they came too near to us. From then on, the *Chulumanos* were a constant presence in my life."

"You saw them every day?" asked the florid man.

"Nearly every day, but not on the weekends. Often just for five minutes a few of them would come into my cell and simply walk up and down, swinging strange weapons and looking me over as if measuring me for a suit of clothes."

"But you were never—that is—there was nothing physical."

"Never on me," the man from Bolivia replied. "Perhaps because I had no information. But there was the constant threat, of course, and I overheard it done on the others; it was intended that I should hear, I'm sure. This went on all the time, even on the weekends. It was very terrible. But we won't speak of it." He picked up his napkin.

"Would you say this was *la nouvelle cuisine* or *cuisine minceur?*" the wide-eyed girl asked the hostess.

"Oh—between the two, I guess. Closer to *la nouvelle.*"

"The wine is very good," commented the florid man.

"Let me give you more. I admire you for staying sane through such an ordeal," the host said to the man from Bolivia.

"There were times. Once I was sitting in a room that had nothing in it but a chair. I had been there, alone, for hours and suddenly the door slammed open and about thirty *Chulumanos* burst into the room waving machine guns and rifles and shouting at the top of their lungs. It was so terrifying, so close to what my mind had imagined—no, was *about* to imagine, sitting there—that I forgot to be amazed at the ingenuity and nearly gave in. Another time the prison director himself, that polite charming fellow, woke me suddenly in the middle of the night, asking me in a frantic tone if I was all right, as if something terrible had happened. I said I was, but he insisted I get out of bed so he could see for himself. At moments like those I almost went over the edge, I can tell you."

The hostess sighed. Four of the guests, by coincidence, reached for their wineglasses and raised them to their lips at exactly the same second. "Let me clear," said the host. The florid man leaned across the table.

"What was he like, the prison director?"

"He was like I have said: charming, urbane, polite. He had a nice family and was devoted to classical music. He was also in charge of all torture, psychological and physical, in the prison."

"But—damn it—that's a cliché!" said the florid man.

"Most cliché's are true," the hostess reminded him.

"Perhaps he means that there is a particular English idiom that expresses the situation," smiled the man from Bolivia. He poked a fork into his salad, beet and endive with shining green curls of chicory. The endive leaves were arranged like spokes around a center of beet and chicory.

"The shoemaker's children have no shoes," said the wide-eyed girl.

"No, no, that's all wrong, that's awful."

"What does it mean? I never did know," said the host.

"Mrs. Jellybye in *Bleak House*, the one who's so busy saving the world while her own children are neglected and miserable."

"But it doesn't apply. It's not right."

"It could be there are no idioms that apply," suggested the man from Bolivia. "I'm a great admirer of Dickens, by the way," he told the wide-eyed girl.

"He's right, there aren't any. 'When in Rome' isn't right. Or 'People who live in glass houses'—"

"Oh, please!"

"How well did you actually know this director?"

"Fairly well. He was my friend, you might say. By coincidence we had known each other at boarding school when we were young. We came from a common tradition."

The hostess, walking away from the table, turned. "Oh, that's too strange!"

"Yes it is. I thought so too," agreed the man from Bolivia.

"Was he an older boy, a bully? Or a new boy? Someone from the lower classes?" Dickens still hung in the air.

"Nothing like that. We were just schoolmates, equals, not compatible but not terrible dissimilar either, except that I was from a left-wing family. No, of course it's strange, the entire two months were strange; the way I was arrested 'out of the blue,' then suddenly one afternoon released just as arbitrarily. The director, by the way, bid me a very charming good-bye that day, over a cup of tea. I learned to accept strangeness, it's how I survived, and I accept it still. I accept that this strange man's life is bound up with my own, that when I return I will see him again. Look at this, how pretty!"

The hostess had brought out the dessert, a trio of homemade sherbets, grapefruit, lime, and mango. There was a vague restless stir among the guests as if some had hoped that the relentless perfection of *la nouvelle* might relax into a rich gooey dessert. The man from Bolivia continued to gaze at the sherbets clustered like a bouquet in dishes with scalloped edges.

"How pretty," he said again.

"Did your wife and children get out all right?"

"Yes, thank you. They will come here next week."

"But—did I understand you?—did you say that you yourself might return some day?" asked the estranged man in a voice barely above a whisper.

"Yes, I will. It's my country. I feel that very strongly."

"I don't see it," said the florid man.

"I can't explain."

"I often think if things got very bad here many people would stay on longer than they had to, simply to keep their apartments," said the host.

"Do you have rent control?" asked the wide-eyed girl.

"Stabilization."

"I can't explain it, but I think there may come a time when some of you will understand," said the man from Bolivia.

"I never will," said the wide-eyed girl.

"Do you want coffee? I'm sorry, we have only decaffeinated," said the hostess.

Nobody wanted coffee. One or two people switched to brandy; the rest stayed with the wine, a cool soft California white. The last of the sunset flowed through a window with hanging plants behind the hostess's chair, falling diagonally across the table to the estranged woman, glancing off pools of melted sherbet. A breeze started up. The host opened another bottle of wine with a small pop.

SEVEN POEMS

ENRIQUE LIHN

Translated from the Spanish by Jonathan Cohen and David Unger

DUMPING GROUNDS

The personnel on this street never changes:
the cast of whores squanders its last penny on make-up
under a grimy light that sticks to their faces.
A double row of decay, houses crumbling like teeth
is the scene for this Dance of Death
dull Saturday boogie in the boil which is the city.

It's a well-known face, covered with seams and black-and-blue
    scars under a few pennies of rouge, which surfaces
    from all the cracks
of the city, in a much older part of town than the
    Alchemists' Quarters:
a snail's bodiless face on the make with the two sexes
    of its androgynous neck
a half-erect phallus smeared with vaginal drool
the bust of a fighter who shows his tits at the entrance
    of a tunnel.

The river doesn't ebb or flow in this dull, boiling
    stretch near the floodgate

The broken springs of a watch hang like fish guts
on the night table
among the curls of a wig dyed pink
The scum of time's waters coiling around
    the rubbish like a snail in its shell
the ecstasy of something that rots once and for all.
[DU]

IN THE SUBWAY STREAM

You never see the same face twice
in the subway stream
Millions of planktonlike faces that sink into the flashing
    in the dark
or that crystallize when struck
by an ad's cold light
at either end of the unknown.
[JC]

OLD LADY ON THE SUBWAY

Her skin arleady in rags and wrapping her flesh
crumples as if it were stuffing or sawdust.
Her head hangs down from her neck, now stiff
and curved like a handle; yet she rides on the subway
at speeds that she couldn't imagine
letting this need carry her, half asleep
clinging to her belongings
bundles whose weight moors her to herself,
bundles half empty, packed more with papers than things.
As every day she's made up for arriving
awake at another station of night
painted with the pink and white tones of a fresh
lilac, this flower of death
Destiny fulfilled yet steadfast
moving from place to place

toward a street at the end of the earth
some Welfare Hotel on Broadway:
a gravelike bed
for dying in this life.

[JC]

HYPERMANHATTAN

This city with its arrogant beggars
is written for others,
and I'm the illiterate one
(the Fates cut me off from English at birth)
going down Fifth Avenue, Manhattan's river
of sharp wind
I'm a handful of words to read
a leaf reading its landscape of letters,
a drifter, swept away by the wind.

If heaven on earth were just as hard
to read, I'd prefer hell
to this noisy land that never breaks
its silence, in Babel.

[JC]

VERSES TO ILLUSTRATE PHOTOGRAPHS FROM SAN ANTONIO DE ATITLÁN

For Francisco Alvarado, the photographer

On Lake Atitlán's shore, the promised land
still sends out a few recognizable sparks:
the two or three electric lights

of San Antonio Palopó, a village where some Cachiquele
families live
Dry clay roofed houses slant down or up from the lake,
since everything revolves
around that one center: the lake
a well girded by mountains and holding the days and the nights
A few shacks looking all alike
as if born from the same mother: the Virgin
House of clay, whitened with lime,
both protected and protecting.

Lake Atitlán revolves, set in motion by Indians rowing
toward the next village, it's the wheel
of fortune where
the rowing farmers trade
their peppers and onions
for ten-gallon hats and flashing strings of beads,
burning their fingers just for a second
on the *quetzales* earned in a day
before they start the dangerous trip back (the Atitlán waters
churn up as the sun drops, failing to pierce them,
the sun that sets high up in the mountains).

The Indians know little about electricity and nothing about
drinking water
hand-woven costumes are their pride
long blue skirts for the women
short skirts for the men
You will know them by their clothing anywhere in Guatemala
and know that they're not far from home
The women's *huipiles* are loose. They do and they don't conceal
their breasts
that they show yet hide in a hardly enticing double form
always within reach of their offspring
Those glistening necklaces
green and yellow paste jewelry coiled around the necks
of all the girls in town no matter how old
from the cradle to the grave
And where are those hats from?

But the necklaces are for women and hats for men
and both symbols set apart the San Antonio natives
from the other Guatemalan Indians
that don't live too far from the U.S.
or too close to the approaching highway that's inching from town
to town around the lake
bringing the message from civilization:
a bunch of tourists.
That highway snakes along six thousand feet above the lake,
each summer drawing a bit closer to San Antonio
which waits very innocently
for temptation to come
It, brag the men, *will save us the work of crossing the lake*
in our canoes
to reach the San Lucas Toliman market
But the highway will save them the work of being themselves
It will happen gradually at first, without their realizing
it and then
so rapidly that no one will remember it.

[DU]

FOR ANDREA

The caterpillar is a tireless worker, it kills
with its unending hunger the few hundred leaves
that a tree, taking pity, holds out to this blind traveler
to help it cross the street.
Holes are all it leaves behind, as this postcard points out.
But the butterfly springs from its cocoon
at the moment of its transfiguration
and she opens the fake eyes of her wings to the light
like an arrow shot forth at birth, but
maybe not her eyes, because she is also blind.
With her artist's wings she dances
like a gypsy to Hungarian violins
never stopping on the same flower twice.

The butterfly forgets it was a caterpillar
just as a caterpillar can't see himself becoming a butterfly
because the two ends of the same being never meet.
[DU]

NEW YORK CATHEDRAL

From which icy planet did this meteor fall
not to have God's mark anywhere on it?
Even if no one still proves God's existence
standing beside this enormous Gothic stage,
it's unnecessary to curb the desire to do it.
The world's largest cathedral has been empty
ever since its one purpose was to be the biggest:
the competitive society's
fruit—huge, but tasteless—
the pious hope of trying to build
a roomy branch of heaven in New York.

Unconfessed ironies crying out to heaven,
Puerto Rican and Harlem blacks
living off the Church's profits
thus reducing it.
They're the unwilling tenants
of St. John's oldest properties
who play their bongos the whole blessèd night
below the dark, confused rose window:
the eye pecked out by dancing crows.
[DU]

FOG

RUSSELL HALEY

Simon Fesk's mother had a sense of humor. There was no denying that. She was seventy-five years old and still wrote to him when she believed the occasion significant. These times were not always personal though they often were. Once she wrote to him on Armistice Day: "Imagine all the silent people," she said. Another time he received a telegram on *her* birthday which simply read: "But for me."

Today was his birthday. He thought of it as halfway to ninety. His mother, though, felt differently. The home-made card stood on the side table.

That is less than an exact description. The card could not stand by itself. It was not made from paper stiff enough to support an upright position. It leaned idly against a milk bottle, insolently concave—a spiv of cards with its trilby hat tipped over its eyes working out a paper deal. A breeze could set it flapping around the rented room.

Nor was the table an ideal surface. He had bought the thing knocked down in both senses, at an auction in Karangahape Road. The legs were shaped like the side frames of a lyre, and they slotted into grooves on the underside of the top. A smaller shelf fitted near the feet and prevented the legs from splaying or collapsing inwards. The surface of the top was carved with jungle blossoms of an unknown species and of such high bas-relief and low intaglio that even the milk bottle was unstable.

Fesk bought it because he liked the color—dark honey. He also needed a table. Simon had a streak of practicality.

Such was the form of the card. Its contents were no less pliable.

"Think only of the future," his mother wrote. "You have your whole young life ahead of you." The card was quarto size, folded once across the center. These words were written in pencil on the front. His mother's hand was still firm. Inside, however, were two printed charts.

A physical impatience welled inside Fesk. He was sitting in his old brown uncut moquette armchair. The chair was also from an auction. It rattled and chimed mysteriously whenever it was moved. No doubt it contained treasures of small change, lost pens, shopping lists. Fesk did not feel this impatience in his head. It stemmed from his legs. He raised his feet in turn from the carpet as though he were walking in a crouch and then he squeezed his thigh muscles. He wore Donegal tweed trousers. Fesk bought them in a mission shop.

They were not charts. Inside the card were two tables. If he had been in a better mood he might have laughed. A thin card containing two printed tables slumped on his decisively carved table.

He did smile. His eyes lit up. Simon forgot his legs. His impatience ceased to exist. Like the tree in the forest which falls unseen and unheard. So large in this country that you could make a whole house from one of them. But people would have to come in and out of doors and switch on radios.

Table One described the various classes of fog signals in use on the 1st of January, 1910, in certain countries. Fesk's own adopted country was not mentioned. As far as fog was concerned this country might not have existed in 1910. Hundreds of years of Polynesian voyaging had been made in the clear sunlight of the Pacific. New Zealand was not tabulated. Fog was infrequent in Auckland though it existed in the thermal areas. Perhaps too in the Marlborough Sounds. Fesk's meteorology was sketchy. So too his geography. He had sailed here on a ship which took many weeks to arrive. Since then he had not moved. His memories of Suez and Aden were dim and blurred. He could not remember whether he saw the Bitter Lakes first or the Red Sea. There was an image of the heat-hazed coastline of North Africa.

But in this table England, Scotland, Ireland, France, the United

States, and British North America were fully examined in terms of fog and signals: sirens, diaphones, horns, trumpets, whistles, explosive devices, guns, bells, gongs, and submarine bells.

To lie there underwater and listen to bells—undersea Sunday—aqua-Christmas!

1910 must have been a festive year if foggy. His mother would have been six years old. He thought of her as a small girl called Lydia clutching a penny. Her maiden name was Martello. But she was born in Ravensthorpe far away from these detailed sea signals. Almost as far away from the sea as you could get in England. Unlike here where he could look out to the islands and the gulf if he opened his curtains.

But the local blanket mill did fire a cannon at ten o'clock every evening fog or no fog. It was called the ten o'clock gun. You could set your watch or close a pub by it. And hooters signaled lunch.

Perhaps she married his father because of the gun—future nostalgia. He was a sailor—shipped out of Hull for Rotterdam and Antwerp. Maybe this card came from his prodigious papers. With senility he had lost the ability to control them. Instead, he grew massive sunflowers in the narrow garden of the new bungalow.

Last Christmas his mother sent him a clipping from the local newspaper. His father, lined beyond comprehension, pouring the dregs of his tea on the earth at the foot of the sunflowers. She wrote a different message then: "Keep us always in mind."

Fesk kept them in his head. Where else? They were his prototypes for the future. Though he would have no children to send clippings and obscurities.

His birthday came in cold weather in this country. If he'd remained in Ravensthorpe it would occur in summer. Impossible to blow out the breath like this and make a small cloud of mist. Bigger there then at eleven and a half, winter, a plume from your lips. Adding minutely to the fog bank which obscured the poplars on the boundary of the football field. Thicker and closer than that suggested. Run three paces and lose yourself. Or your friends. Screaming in wet wool.

"Nobody can get me!" Lighting a tab with his last match. Woodbine smoke and breath pouring from both nostrils. Perfect freedom.

His cat jumped up on the arm of his chair. It ripped at the upholstery and then forced its head against his hand. There were beads of moisture on its whiskers. Titus turned his head as though it were articulated on a ball joint. The underside of his chin was white. Ten. Close to senility.

"Grow flowers," Fesk said. He prodded the cat, and it jumped to the floor. Titus landed awkwardly.

Halfway to ninety. Two thirds of the way to nothing. The last fog. Lying there in your cold sheets with the room dissolving.

There was an unclear patch already. In the top corner of the living room where last winter's rain soaked through obscuring the pattern of the wallpaper. It looked like a small cloud. Miniature gun, diaphone, or bell? Some tiny warning signal: bank—hraarnm—ting!

But perfect freedom. The field like iron. They did that game with breathing. Deep. Deep—sucking in the fog. Then hold it with Wally squeezing his chest. Fooo! Falling forwards on hands and knees with the world crashing. Rehearsals.

It was bigger, that blurred patch. A slide of mucus in his eye. It moved when his gaze altered.

Fesk got up and bathed his eyes in warm water at the sink. He put the kettle on for tea then went to the table to reread the card.

According to Sir Boverton Redwood (1904), duplex burners which give a flame of 28 candle-power have an average oil consumption of 50 grains per candle per hour.

Grains of oil! Solidified fog. You could reverse anything with words. His mother implanting him in the past. The cat sailing up from the floor, its startled look turning to placidity. The head turning. The white chin. Striations in the moquette fading.

Steam issued from the spout of the kettle. Simon knew less about physics than the little he retained of geography. But he remembered that certain bits of the water were agitated and changed their form. Slow them down, and they turn to ice. Tea does not taste the same at the top of Everest. Water boils quicker and colder. So the tea fails to mash, to draw.

He drank his cup in his chair. A knowing smile passed over his face.

She was a cunning old bugger. Fog itself was the warning. Not the signals. She was telling him about change, mutability: fog was the future. Everything gone out of shape. A low ceiling.

He had once caught a bus in thick fog. So dense that the conductor walked ahead, showing the driver the way. And the passengers trudged behind. Walking to keep warm and following the bus so that they did not lose their way. He'd paid full fare. Sixpence to walk!

Whatever light Sir Boverton tried to cast we were walking into darkness. Follow the bus.

It was late now but Simon did not turn on his light. A cruise ship hooted three times as it left the harbor. He had seen flying fish, an albatross, dolphins. The stern and a white trail blazed across the sea. You have been there. You leave your own wake.

After he left home he moved to London. In those days fog was green and frequent. He lived in Archway. Could walk to Hampstead Heath. The fogs drove him wild with desire. He was young. The possibility was held out of meeting a fellow-soul in the fog. Lighted windows took on a special diffuse quality. You could draw close. Who curtained against that blanket?

The city changed shape and decayed under that floor of fog. Lagan to be retrieved in discrete fragments of treasure. A girl dressed in mist—her hair like dark water.

Meetings were an astonishment—looming, distorted, and immediate. And people talked excitedly, their breath catching.

"Are you there? Are you there?"

"Where am I?"

"Haa! I thought I was nearly home."

"Is this the curb?"

"I've passed that corner three times."

And were there really smudge pots burning in the roads? One could walk naked and undetected.

There were more deaths. The old and frail gave up when their boundaries dissolved. They simply merged with whatever was to come. Their bits vibrating in a different mode. Passing out into something else. Steam or ice.

The young survived. They kept their shape because their memories were sharper. Matter is solidified memory of form. In fog a key which had been too long a key could slip its form and run as a bright trickle of amnesia down the thigh. So the old flew out from there. Officials called it pneumonia or influenza.

Fesk knew now that he loved it, fog, as some men love danger. He should not have washed his eyes although the room was comfortingly dark now. It was a poor simulation, but it would have to serve. He should be colder than he was, his skin transparent to the air.

Simon removed everything he had on and sat in his armchair, nude.

Rather than take those sounds as warnings, one could orchestrate them into a hymn in praise of fog:

Boom crack wheeep bong ding blah hoooo
dong fooo crash ting boom wheee!

Repeat and vary. A fifty-grain candle burning as an offering.

Finally Simon knew what he was celebrating. He would leave this meridian of sun where fog, at the very best, came three times a year. He would seek out some industrial valley in a northern clime where factory chimneys poured out their libations to invisibility. Perhaps Ravensthorpe if it had not been ruined by the Clean Air Act.

Certainly not that bright little suburb on the outskirts of York where sunflowers grew in profusion. It would have to be a mucky place where dark bricks absorbed acid from the air. Where the skin was an osmotic device and not a dry barrier tanned and leathered by the sun.

She had made him homesick after all these years.

He would find desire again. One evening. Some dark girl in a mackintosh. Walking huddled streets glazed with rain, inundated with mist.

Fesk sang, the old song, before he retired:

Oh I am a bachelor and I live all alone
And I work at the weaver's trade
And the only only thing I ever did wrong
Was to woo a fair young maid.
I wooed her in the winter time
And in the summer too
And the only only thing I ever did wrong
Was to save her from the foggy foggy dew.

He straightened the card against the milk bottle. It bent again. A meniscus of hope.

Before Simon went to bed he emptied the tea pot outside the

back door. He flung the soggy leaves against the agapanthus growing there.

Somewhere or other his father smiled a blank bright unimpassioned smile. His mother prepared a congratulatory sheet.

Fog descended immediately on all points.

SIX DRAWINGS

VICTOR HUGO

Introduced by Aleksis Rannit

Victor Hugo's Night-Fallen Line

Aleksis Rannit

For Lowry Nelson, Jr.

1.

It was the beginning of May, 1949. Parisian boulevards were awash in an insouciantly reddish sea of flowering horse chestnuts, but even more alluring were the chestnut-tree canvases exhibited at the Durand-Ruel Gallery, painted by that lovely, uneven artist Auguste Renoir. We were sitting in the Café Les Deux Magots. The sky was clear and sculptural, and yet the color of the light was, strangely, that chalky old-fashioned saffron hue favored by Puvis de Chavannes. As always, we spoke of art and poetry, and this time Victor Hugo's name was often on our lips. Looking across the street and seeing early roses in full bloom in the churchyard of Saint-Germain-des-Prés, I started to reconstruct in my memory Hugo's "Chanson," that natural, unhurried song of firm musical close which he wrote in his English exile, but I could recall correctly only one stanza:

—Je pense
aux roses que je semai.
Le mois de mai sans la France
ce n'est pas le mois de mai.

I thought how unfortunate it was that we had lost this luxury of simplicity, and my eye was caught by the street sign for the tiny rue Bonaparte to the left of the little square. I muttered to my friends: "Isn't it paradoxical that there is no one single boulevard or avenue named in honor of Napoleon?" In fact, I was thinking how sad *Hugo* would have been to discover this—he, who with his lyrico-dramatic organ-voice sang the measureless praises of Napoleon I and his luckless son, but who courageously called Napoleon III, then at the height of his power, "Napoléon le Petit."

Who were the "we" sitting in the Café Les Deux Magots?—"We" were the lyrists Jacques Audiberti and Adrien Miatlev (editor of the poetry magazine *La Tour de Feu*), the Estonian etcher-engraver Eduard Wiiralt, Jean Cocteau, and myself.

Two days before, Audiberti had told me a curious story about the prestigious Pléiade anthology of French poetry edited by André Gide, a book which was scheduled to be launched the day of our conversation in the café. In his introduction, Gide devoted many negative pages to Hugo but included not a single one of his poems in the anthology. Gallimard, the publisher, issued an ultimatum, and Gide with ill grace agreed to put in a large group of Hugo's poems but without altering his critical remarks. I am not sure that the selection he made was serious, for most of the texts are merely excerpts. Showing me an advance copy of the anthology, Audiberti had delivered a fiery, hour-long eulogy of Hugo, which he concluded by shouting: "Who is this Gide to belittle Victor Hugo? Without Hugo there would be no Baudelaire, no Verlaine, Rimbaud, Apollinaire, Claudel, not even my own poetry!" Now, meeting in the café, Audiberti asked Cocteau his current opinion of Hugo. Cocteau answered playfully: "I have said it before—that Victor Hugo was a fool who believed that he was actually Victor Hugo—and I have nothing to add to it." I looked at Cocteau, marveling in envy at his very long, delicate bluish-gray scarf (I have always had affection for his poetry, especially for his collection *Plain Song*), but I thought that this time his *bon mot* was rather flat. Audiberti did not respond. It was nearing five o'clock, and he suggested that he and I go together to the *vernissage* of Gide's anthology, and so we went to Gallimard's elegant headquarters, where nearly seventy people were assembled to listen to Gide and, some of them, to ask for his autograph. Gide's *causerie* was skeptical, keen witted, and based on the lengthy prologue to his anthology. After his talk, Marcel Arland, knowing the answer, asked him: "Dear Gide, you have meditated so much on the development of French poetry. Who in your judgment is France's greatest poet?" Gide gave him a lightning answer: "Victor Hugo, alas!" There was laughter and applause. Audiberti's face turned pale, and he seemed about to protest. I grasped his hand and asked him not to. He quit the room saying something I did not catch.

A year later, in the summer of 1950, I met André Gide at the top of the legendary Lorelei cliff on the Rhine. The occasion was a production by the Théâtre National Populaire of Kleist's *The Prince of Homburg*, with the princely Gérard Philipe in the main role. I asked Gide if he still had the same low view of Hugo. "Yes," he asserted categorically, "I do not like emotionalists." I tried to soften the conversation and complimented him on the stylistic fineness of his essay in the anthology. "Oh, no," he replied, "it is just a little thing. Actually, I wrote it in a *pissoir*." And he turned away. It crossed my mind that such things can be said lightheartedly only by the French.

Some ten years afterward I heard from the critic Wladimir Weidlé that it was not Gide but Paul-Jean Toulet who, as early as 1911, made that famous pronouncement: "Victor Hugo, alas!" Was this the reason Gide included Toulet, a minor poet, in his anthology yet excluded many remarkable masters, among them the poet of high solitude, O.V. de L. Milosz, whom Kenneth Rexroth rescued for the English-speaking world in 1952?

2.

Today—that is, since about 1960—Victor Hugo has no need of defenders of his literary art (who knows what may happen to him in the next century?). He has returned triumphant, especially as a poet. His critics finally understand that, with his instinctive revolt against the pseudoclassical rigor—the language having gone flat—of the Empire's *verse-gardens*, it was he who created a new French poetry, poetry that is a form of singing. Now he is glorified by the French even more fervently than we on these shores exalt the newly reborn Walt Whitman, whom Helen Vendler lately proclaimed "the greatest American poet." (Is the accent on "American" or on "poet"?) Hugo may *even* be superior to Whitman, because whatever the Dionysian content of his saturated yet luminous poems, he knew how to create an immutable marriage between tenderness and manliness of spirit, between sonorous verbal simplicity and the austere fervor of his verse schemes, and he did so with subtlety and variety of power.

The return of Hugo the writer has not helped Hugo the graphic artist, even though for a number of his books, he, in point of fact, first made the drawings and only then began the writing. Recognized as a draughtsman of great talent, he still stands in the shadow of Hugo the man of letters. There are no comprehensive monographs on his art, and there is not even a *catalogue raisonné* of the large corpus of his drawings. The only works which have been investigated seriously are his eccentric architectural compositions, in which he replaced an empirical method of analysis with spontaneous reflection, so that they can be seen as tectonic and symbolic, densely crowded forms *in motion.* And this he did almost a century before Antoni Gaudí. Strangely enough, he never studied painting or drawing, only geometry, being interested principally in the treatment of line as an element of space, and in employing the very notion of geometrical continuity—points and lines at infinity. This study and interest are not immediately apparent in Hugo's graphic work, but it is precisely his secret mathematical comprehension of linear form, combined with an instinctive mastery of spatial cognition, that makes his drawings strong, uniting a kind of Mediterranean perfection of structure with a bizarre, Gothic intensity of pathos. This candid synthesis is manifested throughout his work even when he is caught up in the most phantasmal intoxication. In consequence, Hugo's work is obsessed by a Manichean dualism. The musical and the dramatic, gloomy sublimity and grotesque orgy, the real and the unreal are at grips with one another and result in what he himself called the harmony of "white and black rays." His luxuriously painterly ink drawings of landscapes are bathed in that double-faced light which also veraciously reflects his favorite adjectives: *perilous, startling, uncanny, beastly, creepy, livid, ghastly, deformed, funereal.*

Two years ago, nine of Hugo's disturbing and surprising drawings, now in the Musée Hugo, were discovered in Paris; from them we select and publish six. All of them are of original and unique mobility, marked by the tremulous delights of a devil incarnate. These powerful effigies probe deeply into the unease of the human state, even more than do Hugo's delirious and lustrous architectural chimeras or his weird somnambulist landscapes in which mountains, rocks, turbulent skies, and seas are already transformed into monsters, spirits, and demons.

Every drawing has its own style, but they are united by unresolved tensions and frustrations; and there is not a single weak rhythmic figure in them. Some of us who admire Matisse's skillful simplicity will read with attention the pencil sketch of a malevolent cat-woman called *Démone vue en rêve* [*Demoness seen in a dream*], in which pleasing and concordant beauty is joined with the emotionally irregular, jagged, and awesome. Others may be taken by his *Dessin rapportant à la sorcière* [*Sketch regarding the sorceress*], in which a Rabelaisian visage may have been translated into the face of a cliff, one of those spectral cliffs which can be seen in Corsica, the place of Hugo's infancy. The drawing has a Picassoidal decorative power, just as some others of Hugo look like Picassos before Picasso. In *Sorcier* [Sorcerer] the kind of proto-Redonian distortion of the features of a cannibalistic exorcist, carried by the sinister black areas, are Hugo's chief means of expression. (We may recall Han of Iceland, the satanic bandit in Hugo's romance, who asked pointedly: "Have you ever eaten the entrails of children while they were still alive?") In a stylistically lighter, necromantic *Autoportrait* [*Self-portrait*] (?), fashioned as a large, round form floating in empty space and vibrant with rapidly realized horizontals and semidiagonals, Hugo creates a half comic, half ill-starred, realistic image of a hell-born grimacer's self-dream.

The ultimate masterpieces of this hallucinatory cycle are the *Main bénissante de l'abbesse* [*The blessing hand of the Mother Superior*] and the *Autre juge* [*Another judge*], and I venture to suggest that their artistic and psychographic significance is not below that present in the drawings of Grünewald, Rembrandt, and Goya. Truly Goyaesque is the intense and frightening portrait of the judge; it has also a lightness and fragility of line not known to Goya—a nearly supernatural touch through which *la ligne satanique* of its content changes in the artist's hand into an aesthetic *ligne divine*. Can one imagine that this strong, infinitely frail drawing was realized with a broken match? Yes, the Abstract Expressionists may well envy Hugo, the revolutionary experimentalist; he liked to work with jagged steel pens, crooked iron blades, dirty rags, and unusable brushes, and he mixed black coffee into his India ink to produce what sepia wash could not give him: a muscular, deeply sensual tonality of line and space.

Hugo's *The blessing hand of the Mother Superior*, with its cosmic theatricality, guilty splendor, and purgatorial light, was accomplished with a robust and supple, drastically deformed goose quill. Looking at this drawing one realizes that the "magnanimity" is here a pinnacle of that blessedness which borders on abhorrence and madness. Could any modernist master among the boldest of figurative painters ever hope to recreate a similar lava-slow movement of the hand, transforming ugliness into a Hugolian absolute of expressionistically dynamic beauty?

3.

It is sad to remember that even so cognitive an art critic as Baudelaire, the champion of Delacroix's Romanticism, did not recognize the radical Romanticist aesthetics of the artist Victor Hugo and the anxiety and dangers of his humanity faced with the responsibility of existence. But we may be consoled: another great critic, who was and still is beyond compare in his compassion and precise judgment, called Hugo's drawings "astonishing things" on one occasion and on another termed his art work "grand, immense, infinite." What could one add to those veridical adjectives? —Perhaps only the name of the critic: Vincent Van Gogh.

However lyrical, Hugo's talent is epic in its spectacular onward surge, its terrible sublimity, its more-than-life quality. He was a titan burning not with stolen but with God-given or Satan-given fire of insatiable impulse. According to Hugo's biographers, every morning he composed about a hundred lines of verse (destroying much of it later), made numerous drawings at noontime, regularly wrote twenty pages of prose in the afternoon, and visited his *admiratrices* in the evening. In addition, he loved to do wall painting, carpentry, and upholstering and showed professional skill as a designer, interior decorator, and architect. A society man, he entertained fashionable Paris, took part in spiritualist seances, was a fervent traveler, a passionate politician, but also a devoted father to his children and an ardent friend of many writers and artists. —Was he in his art, like Grünewald and Goya, a precursor standing before, above, and beyond modernist form-experience? Do his accomplishments as a graphic artist come up to what Léon-Paul Fargue said about him as a poet in 1947? —"Hugo is one who will penetrate the future."

Victor Hugo liked to use the image of an "eagle hovering above the eternal depths." Is he himself a still unmeasured, stormy, untypically Gallic eagle? A Gothic Goethean eagle? Does he in his esoteric art, in his psychosensorial prose, in the visuality of all his arts, possess the French, or rather Germanic, "world-soul?" Is Hugolian Romanticism not art as the living form of *feeling*, as we have thought before, but art as the powerful, open form of *thought?*

Victor Hugo's unpublished preface to these drawings reads as follows:—Pièces du procès. / Portraits authentiques / de divers diables / que la sorcière / a eu / le tort / de trigauder [*Sketches of the trial. / Authentic portraits / of various devils / whom the sorceress / made the mistake / of cheating*]

Démone vue en rêve [*Demoness seen in a dream*]. Pencil drawing. *C.* 1850. Photo Bulloz, Paris.

Dessin rapportant à la sorcière [*Drawing regarding the sorceress*]. Charcoal drawing. *C.* 1850. Photo Bulloz, Paris.

Sorcier [*Sorcerer*]. Brush drawing and wash. *C.* 1850. Photo Bulloz, Paris.

Autoportrait [*Self-portrait*] (?). Pencil drawing. *C.* 1850. Photo Bulloz, Paris.

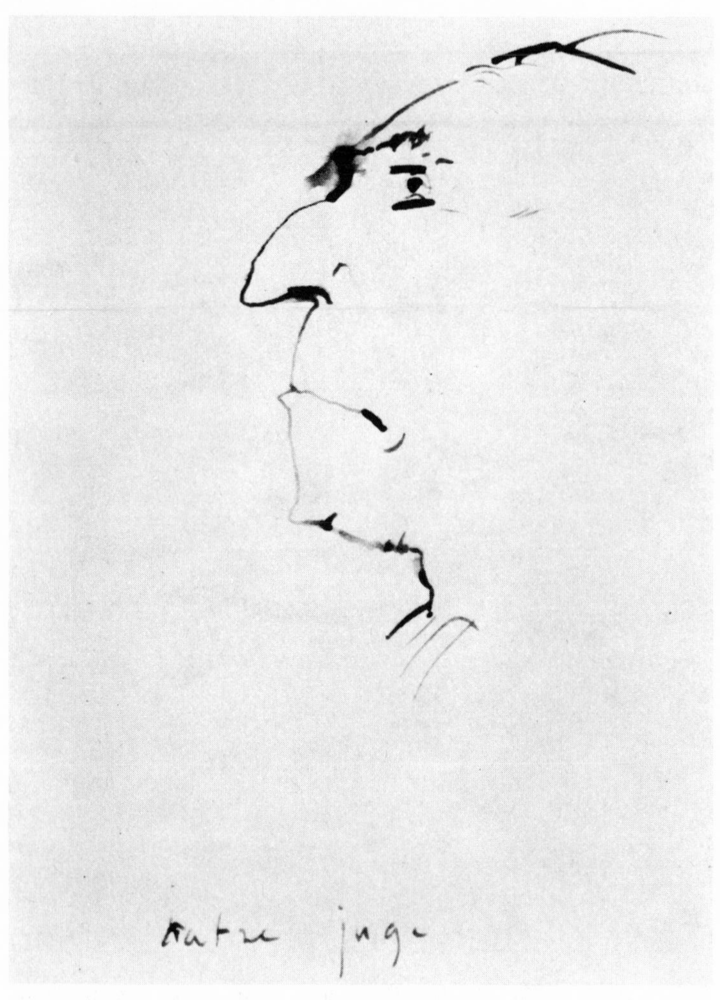

Autre juge [*Another judge*]. India ink drawing. *C.* 1850. Photo Bulloz, Paris.

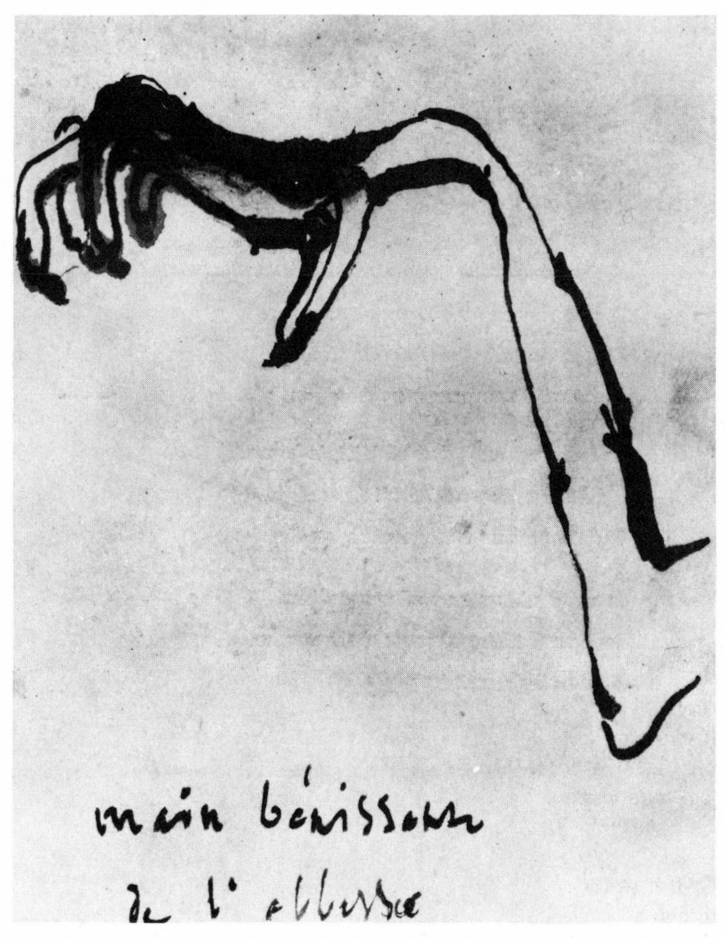

Main bénissante de l'abbesse [*The blessing hand of the Mother Superior*]. Goose quill drawing. *C.* 1850. Photo Bulloz, Paris.

TWO POEMS

DENNIS LEE

AS SHE GROWS OLDER

(For a mean old lady; and for those who have to watch)

If you went gent-
ly miss-
ing, like a lawnful of
dew at
dawn saying, "No,
no, there's a boy still asleep, let him come to
his skin his own his early
skin, the one that can
tingle;
bring him to me, let me show him
the meaning of footprints;
five minutes then
I'm gone—"

Or if it were
indigo
sky with somehow a bruise of acceleration:
great light/gratuitous
blackout, yes too soon but who

kept time at all? at all? a
flex in the order of things, and really a quantum riff,
release of the gathered—

Or if, with an
in-
finite gesture of
solace you
said, "I know, I
know," and
you knew;
and then you
settled, while we
still saw, into an
otherness that we were nearly too close to remember to feel
    spooked by.

DOWNWARD OF ROSES

Downward of Roses,
scumward of oceans of whales, darkward of stars:
deathward dimension of every substantial thing—

did you not have dominion enough? do men have to lend a hand?

THE BROOKLYN BRANDING PARLORS

JAMES PURDY

are a temple of torture
their address changes nightly
young men go there to prove their manhood
the master of the place wears a mask
the exposed parts of his body appear to be stained with
    walnut juice
though perhaps he is black
his eyes alone are fairly visible
they shoot fire but don't look in-sane
The penitent is tied to an iron halter
& chooses the instrument of his pain:
hot irons or the whip,
or if he thinks he is a hero, both.
even though the sufferer is gagged
his screams of bloody murder
reach the outdoors.
hence the parlors change their site nightly
like a wandering medicine show.
I wonder, Do they exist?
If not why do men go on talking about them?

NOTES ON CONTRIBUTORS

JOHN ALLMAN's *Walking Four Ways in the Wind* was published in 1979 by Princeton University Press in the Princeton Series of Contemporary Poets. He is currently at work on a new collection, *Dostoevsky at Semyonov Square*. Seven of his poems appeared in *ND40*.

For the past forty years, the poetry of JOÃO CABRAL DE MELO NETO has strongly influenced poetics and metaphysics in his native Brazil. He is best known for his verse-play *Morte E Vida Severina*, and for "Uma Faca Só Lâmina" ("A Knife All Blade"). His book *A Escola das Facas* (*"The School for Knives"*) came out in Brazil in 1981. KERRY SHAWN KEYS has published translations from the German and Tamil as well as from the Portuguese. He is the editor and translator of *O Pintor E O Poeta* (*The Painter and the Poet*): *José Paulo Moreira Da Fonesca*, and *Quingumbo: New North American Poetry*, and has three books of original poetry to his credit.

MELINDA CHATAIN has lived in Ireland, Japan, and Canada, and presently resides in New York City. "Account" is her first published story.

ALLEN GROSSMAN was awarded the Witter Bynner Prize by the American Academy of Arts and Letters for *The Woman on the Bridge Over the Chicago River* (New Diretcions, 1979). In 1981, Rowan Tree Press brought out *Against Our Vanishing: Winter Conversations with Allen Grossman on the Theory and Practice of Poetry*, a book of interviews conducted by Mark Halliday. *Of the Great House: A Book of Poems* will be published by New Directions in 1982.

RUSSELL HALEY, whose work also appeared in *ND42* and *ND43*, lives in New Zealand, where his first collection of stories, *The Sauna*

Bath Mysteries, came out in 1978. Earlier publications, of poetry, were *The Walled Garden* (1972) and *On the Fault Line* (1977). He is now working on "Northern Lights," an extended but discontinuous narrative.

A native Californian, MICHAEL HANNON has published poetry in *City Lights Journal #3, Open Space, The San Francisco Oracle,* and other magazines. He is the author of several chapbooks, and small letterpress editions of his work have been published by Turkey Press.

A biography of the noted Imagist poet H. D. (HILDA DOOLITTLE, 1886–1961) by Janice S. Robinson was published by Houghton Mifflin earlier this year. New Directions has brought out three of H. D.'s books of poetry (*Helen in Egypt, Hermetic Definition,* and *Trilogy*) as well as *End to Torment: A Memoir of Ezra Pound,* reminiscences about her lifelong colleague and champion, and most recently, *HERmione,* an autobiographical novel. "Vale Ave" is published here for the first time.

For information on VICTOR HUGO, see Aleksis Rannit's introduction to "Six Drawings." Curator of Russian and East European studies at Yale, ALEKSIS RANNIT is one of the foremost poets in the Estonian language. His work has appeared frequently in these pages.

EDMOND JABÈS was born in Cairo in 1912. As a Jew, he was forced to leave Egypt forty-four years later, during the Suez crisis, and he settled in Paris. When Editions Gallimard brought out the first three volumes of *The Book of Questions* during the 1960s, Jabès was established as one of the major writers in French of our time, and in 1970 he won the coveted Prix des Critics. Books I–III of *The Book of Questions* are available in English translation from Wesleyan University Press; Book V was published by Tree Books. ROSEMARY WALDROP, a professor of English at Tufts University, has translated all of Jabès' work to appear in English. She has written four books of poetry, published by Burning Deck, Open Places, and Seven Woods Press, and a critical study, *Against Language?*, available from Mouton.

DENNIS LEE was born in Toronto in 1939. He has published ten books; the most recent volumes of poetry are *Civil Elegies* and *The Gods.*

Winner of the prestigious Cuban Casa de las Americas Prize in 1966, ENRIQUE LIHN (born 1929) has been acknowledged as one of the leading Chilean poets of his generation. He has published a book of short stories and a novel as well as collections of verse. In 1978, New Directions brought out *The Dark Room and Other Poems.* JONATHAN COHEN translated poems in *The Dark Room* and, more recently, parts of Ernesto Cardenal's *Zero Hour and Other Poems* (New Directions, 1981). A collection of his own poetry, *Poems from the Island,* is available from Street Press. DAVID UNGER's translations also appeared in *The Dark Room.*

MICHAEL MCGUIRE's plays have been produced in San Francisco, Los Angeles, New York, and points in between, as well as abroad. His stories have appeared in *Paris Review* and *The Hudson Review,* and he has lectured on Drama and Creative Writing at universities in the U.S., Canada, and Saudi Arabia. He currently makes his home in Oregon.

Since his first collection of fiction, *Color of Darkness* (New Directions, 1957), JAMES PURDY has been a strong presence on the literary scene. Arbor House has published his recent novels: *In a Shallow Grave* (1976), *Narrow Rooms* (1978), and *The Mourners Below* (1980).

LEONARDO SINISGALLI (born 1908) lives in Rome, where he is an advertising director and graphic arts expert. Besides publishing widely acclaimed books of poetry, stories, and essays, he has had numerous shows of his graphic art. W. S. DI PIERO's poetry and criticism has appeared in *The New Yorker, Canto, Partisan Review,* and many other magazines. His translations of Leopardi and Sandro Penna have been published by Louisiana State University Press and Ohio University Press, and Oxford University Press will be bringing out his collaborative translation (with William Arrowsmith) of Euripides' *Ion.* He was the recipient of the Renato Poggioli Award, administered by PEN American Center, in 1982.

Two books by poet GUSTAF SOBIN are available in the U.S.—a children's book, *The Tale of the Yellow Triangle* (Braziller, 1973), and a collection of poems, *Wind Chrysalid's Rattle* (Montemora Supplements, 1980). His poems have appeared in *ND32, 36,* and 40.

JULIA THACKER has published poetry and fiction in *Antaeus, Mademoiselle, Ms.,* and *The Massachusetts Review,* and her story "In the Glory Land" will appear in *Pushcart Prizes 1981–82*. In 1981, she was a Bunting Fellow in Creative Writing at Radcliffe.

The *Paris Review* Khan Prize for fiction was awarded to PAUL WEST in 1974. His most recent novel, *The Very Rich Hours of Count von Stauffenburg,* was brought out by Harper & Row in 1980.